Junior's voice was abruptly replaced by a dial tone for a moment, and then another line crossed in. Jessica recognized Greenback's voice. As usual, he was giving delivery instructions to somebody—Rock, it sounded like. Jessica didn't pay much attention.

But then something in Greenback's voice made Jessica tune in to his conversation. "I've trusted you with a special job, Rock. She'll be at the usual place." Greenback's voice dropped to a rough whisper. "Make sure you take care of her. Don't disappoint me. Because if they don't find her body floating soon, they'll find *yours*."

Click. Greenback's voice was replaced by a dial tone.

The receiver fell from Jessica's hand onto the desktop with a clatter. She was completely stunned.

Exactly what had she heard this time? Greenback's ominous words came back to her. Jessica shuddered. A floating body . . . Had the two men on the phone been talking about *murder*?

MURDER ON THE LINE

Written by
Kate William

Created by
FRANCINE PASCAL

BANTAM BOOKS
NEW YORK • TORONTO • LONDON • SYDNEY • AUCKLAND

RL 6, age 12 and up

MURDER ON THE LINE

A Bantam Book / December 1992

Sweet Valley High is a registered trademark of Francine Pascal
Conceived by Francine Pascal
Produced by Daniel Weiss Associates, Inc.
33 West 17th Street
New York, NY 10011
Cover art by James Mathewuse

ISBN 0-553-29308-7

Published simultaneously in the United States and Canada

Bantam Books are published by Bantam Books, a division of Bantam
Doubleday Dell Publishing Group, Inc. Its trademark, consisting of the
words ''Bantam Books'' and the portrayal of a rooster, is
Registered in U.S. Patent and Trademark Office and in other
countries. Marca Registrada. Bantam Books, 666 Fifth Avenue,
New York, New York 10103.

PRINTED IN THE UNITED STATES OF AMERICA

OPM   0   9   8   7   6   5   4   3   2   1

MURDER ON THE LINE

One

"It's Friday—finally!" exclaimed sixteen-year-old Jessica Wakefield as she collapsed into the passenger seat of the Jeep she shared with her twin sister, Elizabeth. "I was afraid this week would never end."

Elizabeth laughed. "This is only the second week of our summer internship. How can you be burned out already?"

Jessica stifled a yawn. "I guess boredom has that effect on me."

"*I* think you just don't like to admit that sometimes working can be as much fun as playing! Anyway," Elizabeth said as she turned the Jeep onto Calico Drive, "I think we were lucky to land these internships. We're learning how to research, write, and edit newspaper articles; we're seeing how the whole paper is put together and printed; *and* we're working closely with handsome young editors and reporters!" Elizabeth shot a teasing glance at her sister.

Jessica smiled, her dimple flashing. "I *do* like that last part," she admitted. "I would have quit on the first day if it weren't for Bill. When he looks at me with those gorgeous blue eyes, he can make any assignment sound romantic, even standing at the copy machine!"

Elizabeth had to agree that Bill Anderson, the recently hired news editor who was responsible for overseeing the summer interns working at the *Sweet Valley News*, was very handsome and charismatic. "And he's not just good-looking. He's so smart and creative," she said.

"And sophisticated and well-traveled," Jessica added. "He's lived in so many cool places." She sighed regretfully. "Too bad he's so old."

"Old!" Elizabeth exclaimed. "He's only about thirty!"

"And that's too old for me." Examining herself in the mirror on the back of the sun visor, Jessica fluffed her silky blond hair. "Besides, I'm not positive, but I think he has a girlfriend."

"A girlfriend—oh, no!" Elizabeth teased. "Then you might as well quit. Or are you ready to concede that working at the *News* is a great experience, with or without a cute boss?"

"It's a great way to meet guys," Jessica said

firmly. "And that's the only reason I'm sticking with it. I'll leave the great experience part to you—you actually want to do newspaper work for a *living*." Jessica made a face.

"So you still think lounging by the pool or cruising the mall with Lila would have been a more rewarding way to spend your vacation," Elizabeth commented.

Jessica grinned. "You've got it."

Elizabeth shook her head and laughed. When the end of the school year had found Jessica with no definite summer plans, their parents had encouraged her to sign up for a position at the *News* with Elizabeth, or else look for a full-time baby-sitting job. Jessica had decided on the internship. But it looked as if nothing could change her opinion that a summer job of any kind was just a necessary evil.

The twins' differing attitudes toward employment were only another example of how different they were. Though Jessica and Elizabeth shared a classic California beauty, with their sun-streaked blond hair and slender figures, the resemblance ended there. Jessica lived for the moment; having fun was always her top priority. Elizabeth tended to be more practical and responsible; she enjoyed setting goals and achieving them. While Jessica had already had about a dozen crushes on different guys at the newspaper, Elizabeth was devoted to her steady boyfriend, Todd Wilkins, who was out of town on a camping trip with his parents. In spite of all their differences, though, the Wakefield twins were the closest of friends, and Elizabeth—if not Jessica—was glad that she and her sister were working at the same office this summer.

They drove up to the entrance of the municipal parking garage next to the Western Building, home of the *Sweet Valley News*. "Oh, no. The garage is full again!" Jessica moaned.

"We'll have to look for a spot on the street," said Elizabeth, circling around the block. "What a pain."

Jessica pointed. "There's one!"

Elizabeth quickly pulled into the empty space. As the twins strolled down the sidewalk toward the seven-story Western Building, the rumble of the construction taking place farther down the block filled the air. "That's why it's getting impossible to park in Sweet Valley," Elizabeth said. "All this growth downtown!"

Jessica nodded. A number of new buildings had appeared in Sweet Valley recently. This project, the newest and most extensive yet, was owned by George Fowler, one of the wealthiest businessmen in southern California and the father of Jessica's best friend, Lila. It would be the tallest office tower in town. Jessica put a hand to her mouth and coughed. "Ugh. The dust is terrible!"

"What?" Elizabeth shouted.

They ran into the lobby of the Western Building and waved their employee ID cards at the receptionist. "I said, it's really a mess out there," Jessica complained as she and Elizabeth crossed to the elevator bank.

"When it's finished, it'll be a neat building. Too bad it has to disrupt business all over town in the meantime." Elizabeth stepped into the elevator and pressed the button for the fifth floor. "This thing with the phones at the *News* is really out of control."

When the elevator stopped at their floor, the twins crossed the hall toward the glass door with the words *The Sweet Valley News* painted on it in bold black letters.

The newspaper's receptionist, Rose, stationed just beyond the door, was shouting at someone over the phone. "I don't care what Mr. Fowler says!" Rose's cheeks were pink with fury. "We cannot function if our telephone service is constantly being interrupted. I am bombarded with wrong numbers, and half the extensions in the office aren't working properly."

"Poor Rose," Jessica whispered. "She's going nuts!"

The large, open newsroom, flanked on either side by private offices, was already buzzing with the sounds of talking and typing. "Rose is right! I guess she hasn't figured out yet that it's not going to get her anywhere to complain, even if she *is* justified," said Elizabeth. "Nothing's going to stand in the way of Fowler Tower!"

As the twins headed in the direction of the office they shared, thanks to the temporary absence of a couple of vacationing reporters, Elizabeth was flagged down by Anita Solarz and Seth Miller, the two young reporters she assisted.

Jessica had had a crush on tall, handsome Seth, but had lost interest when she discovered that no amount of eyelash fluttering could distract him from his work, to which he was completely devoted. Seth had an M.A. in journalism and wrote mystery stories in his spare time. Anita, a pretty, petite brunette with boundless energy, was a recent college graduate. Elizabeth looked up to both as role models.

"Liz, can you join me and Seth for a conference in a few minutes?" Anita called. "We want to outline next week's stories."

"I'll be right with you," Elizabeth promised.

"Hey, Wakefields," another voice called out behind them. "Ready to rock and roll?"

Jessica and Elizabeth both turned at the greeting, and Jessica treated Bill Anderson to her most dazzling smile. "Got something fun for me this morning?"

"Do I ever." He tossed her a small cassette tape. "I dictated some story ideas," he told her. "Can you type them up and put them in some kind of coherent order for the story meeting this afternoon?"

Typing, my favorite, Jessica thought disgustedly. But she couldn't resist Bill's disarming grin, and the sexy way he raked his hand through his thick, dark hair sent a tingle down her spine. "I'll get right on it," she promised.

"Thanks, Jess. And Liz," Bill said, training his electric blue eyes on Elizabeth, "you're all set with Anita and Seth, right?"

"Yep," Elizabeth confirmed. "We're about to get to work on next week's stories."

"You two are the best. See you at the two o'clock meeting." With rapid strides, Bill was off to check up on the other interns.

Jessica sank into her chair. Pushing off from her desk, she twirled the chair around on its tiny wheels. "Isn't he incredible?" she asked dreamily.

"I thought he was too old," Elizabeth kidded. She shuffled through the papers on her desk, locating a file she needed for her conference with Anita and Seth. "You know, I feel kind of guilty, Jess. You're stuck typing today while I get to cruise around Sweet Valley with Seth, researching this parking-problem story."

Because of her experience writing for the Sweet Valley High paper, *The Oracle*, Elizabeth's summer assignment was to act as an assistant to Seth and Anita. She got to spend a lot of time out of the office investigating stories while Jessica spent most of her time in the newsroom, helping out in a more general way with editorial and research work and odd tasks.

"I don't mind," Jessica said honestly. And she really didn't. By hanging around the office, she

7

got to see a lot of Bill. Maybe he was too old for her and already had a girlfriend; maybe her crush on him was never going to go anywhere. Still, Bill was more intriguing than the parking problem in Sweet Valley any day!

"I should probably get back to work," Jessica told Lila. "I can't believe you're going shopping in L.A. without me."

"So leave the office early and come with me," Lila suggested.

"Leave early?" Jessica snorted. "I've only been here an hour. No, I'm swamped." She looked at Bill's dictation tape and the pile of proofreading Dan Weeks, one of the reporters, had just dumped on her desk. "See you at the Dairi Burger tonight."

Jessica pressed a button on her phone and hung up on Lila. Then she lifted her finger, preparing to dial Amy Sutton to tell her about the plan to meet at the Dairi Burger. To her surprise, instead of hearing a dial tone she heard a strange woman's voice.

"Hello? Hello?" Jessica said. "Who is this?" The woman went on chattering. Jessica pressed the disconnect button on her phone a few more times, then listened again. The woman was still there! "Who are you?" Jessica cried. "What are you doing on my phone?" The woman just kept gabbing.

Oh, I know, Jessica thought. *It's the stupid, messed-up phone system!*

Jessica slammed down her receiver. How was she supposed to make plans with her friends? For a brief moment she considered storming out and demanding that Rose do something about this inconvenience. And then she caught herself. *Wait a minute,* she thought. *This could be fun!*

She picked up her phone again. Sure enough, the woman was still there. "I just don't know what to do, Dana," the woman wailed. "Frank's always been a good husband. And he gives me anything I want. The other day he came home from work with a sapphire bracelet. It's so heavy that my wrist hurts when I wear it! And it wasn't for any particular occasion. Frank said he bought it because the sapphires reminded him of my eyes."

Jessica smiled. She liked the sound of that. She wouldn't mind having a filthy rich husband who showered her with jewels! What was this woman's problem?

"So why aren't you happy with him, Maggie?" the woman named Dana asked.

"We never have any fun," Maggie explained, sniffling. "He's more than twice my age, you know."

"Ugh!" Jessica said.

"He never wants to go out," Maggie continued, "unless it's to some boring corporate function. He never lets his hair down."

"Maybe because he doesn't *have* any hair," Dana said sarcastically.

Jessica giggled. Maggie blew her nose. "Then there's Craig. He doesn't have a penny to his name, Dana, but he has the *best* body."

Jessica listened eagerly. This was really getting juicy! At that moment, someone standing behind her cleared his throat.

Jessica quickly hung up the phone and spun around, her cheeks flushing guiltily. "It's just me," said Dan Weeks. "I've got one more article for you to proof."

"Oh, I was just getting to your stuff," Jessica said glibly. She grabbed her red pencil. "I'll have it back to you in a jiff."

As soon as Dan left the office Jessica tossed the pencil aside and reached for the phone. But to her disappointment, all she heard was a dial tone—no Maggie and Dana. *Drat*, Jessica thought, jiggling the button on the phone. Suddenly a new stranger's voice came on the line.

"I know, Mother," the man said meekly. "I *could* be making more money. But—"

"Stand up for yourself, Junior!" his mother barked. "You'll never get a promotion if you don't ask for it. Don't you want to move out of that crummy studio apartment?"

"Yes, Mother. But it's all I can afford right now and I really don't need—"

"You need a wife, that's what you need. What happened to that Sharon person?"

"Sharon met someone else," Junior said sadly.

I don't blame her! Jessica thought. *What a wimp!*

"Look, Mother, I have a meeting to get to. I'll call you tonight, all right?"

Jessica listened while Junior's mother made him promise to start taking vitamins and watch his cholesterol intake. As soon as their conversation ended another line crossed in. *Wow,* Jessica thought. *This is really a bonanza!*

"Home Shoppers Club," a man said. "May I take your order?"

"Yes," a woman replied eagerly. "I would like item number two-forty-two—the poodle cardigan, size medium. Six of them, please."

Six poodle cardigans? Jessica thought.

"And the faux pearl necklace and earring set, item number eighty-eight. And the faux ruby butterfly pendant and ring set, item one-seventeen. And the . . ." The woman continued to talk, and Jessica raised her eyebrows. She was a shopaholic herself, but *this* was ridiculous.

"What on earth are you listening to?"

The unexpected sound of Elizabeth's voice made Jessica jump. She replaced the receiver. "You're not going to believe this, Liz! All I have to do is pick up my phone and I can hear other people's conversations without them knowing it!"

Elizabeth raised her eyebrows. "You're *eavesdropping?*"

Jessica smiled. "Yes, and it's a riot. You should hear what some of these people talk about! One woman just blew about a thousand bucks ordering the tackiest things from the Home Shoppers Club. Six poodle cardigans! And a woman named Maggie is not at *all* happy with her husband, Frank," Jessica babbled. "He's twice her age *and* a real bore. She's thinking of fooling around with some hunk named Craig—he has a great body, but not a lot of cash. I didn't get the whole scoop. And a guy called Junior really has to do something about his mother. He lets her boss him around as if he were still a little boy!"

Elizabeth shook her head indulgently. "I can't believe you actually spent your morning this way."

"Spent my morning . . . ?" Jessica glanced at the clock over the door. "Wow, time flies when you're having fun!" she said.

Elizabeth sat down at her desk on the other side of the room and switched on her computer. "It's all the same to me, Jess," she said over her shoulder. "But for your own sake, you might consider doing a little work for a change. Bill won't be too happy if you're not prepared for the story meeting this afternoon."

Dutifully, Jessica popped the cassette into the dictaphone and typed a few words on her computer keyboard. But as soon as she saw that Elizabeth was completely absorbed in her own typing, Jessica quietly removed the earphones and reached for the telephone.

Elizabeth was probably right; she usually was.

But since when did Jessica ever take her twin's sensible advice? *I deserve a little fun*, Jessica thought, lifting the telephone receiver to her ear.

Great! It was Maggie again! "You've got to tell me what to do, Wendy," Maggie begged. "Do I stay with Frank or run off with Craig?"

Jessica grinned. No two ways about it—the crazy phone situation that was inconveniencing so many of her fellow employees just might make *her* boring job a little more interesting!

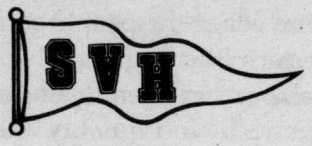

Two

"Rose said she's been getting crossed calls from other offices in the building. So I bet my callers are from the Western Building, too." Excitedly, Jessica waved her sandwich in the direction of a red-haired woman in a green silk dress who had just walked out of the Western Building. "Do you think that's Maggie? Or maybe that is, over there." She elbowed Elizabeth. "Look, Liz. Do you think *that* could be her?"

"How should I know?" Elizabeth asked.

It was lunch hour on Monday and the twins were sitting on a bench outside the Western Building, on the opposite side from where the construction was taking place. It was a typically bright and beautiful California day, and ordinar-

14

ily Jessica would have been working on her tan, her face tipped to the sun. But she wasn't about to close her eyes today. She was having too much fun speculating about the people walking in and out of the Western Building.

Jessica bit into her chicken salad sandwich. She chewed and swallowed quickly, then elbowed Elizabeth again. "How about that guy, Liz? That scrawny guy with the wire-rimmed glasses. I bet that's Junior, the one with the nagging mom."

"Yeah, maybe that's Junior," Elizabeth said without raising her eyes from the computer printout she was reading.

"You didn't even look at him," Jessica complained.

"Sorry, Jess. I just have other things to think about."

"Like what?"

"Like trying to cut enough words from this story so it will fit into two columns in the newspaper."

Jessica looked over Elizabeth's shoulder. The story was about a benefit to raise funds for a new wing at the Sweet Valley public library. Jessica could not believe Elizabeth found that more interesting than guessing the identities of the people Jessica had been eavesdropping on. Elizabeth really took this internship thing too seriously!

"Just cut out all the long words," Jessica suggested. "The ones with more than two syllables."

Elizabeth laughed. "Thanks for the tip."

Jessica resumed watching the entrance of the Western Building. She narrowed her eyes at a glamorous woman in a hot pink dress. "Now *she* looks like someone who'd be married to a rich guy and thinking about having an affair," she commented. "I bet she's sneaking off to meet Craig right now!"

As if on cue, an incredibly gorgeous guy in khakis and a striped oxford shirt approached the Western Building. He was tall, blond, tanned, and handsome. Jessica's jaw dropped. *If that's Craig, I'd tell Maggie to go for it!*

It wasn't Craig. Without even a glance at the woman in pink, the young man walked purposefully past her—and headed right for Jessica and Elizabeth!

Quickly, Jessica sat up straight. She tossed back her hair and lifted her chin, ready to catch his eye and flash him her most captivating smile.

"Who are you staring at?" Elizabeth wanted to know. "You don't think *he's* Junior, do you?"

"Of course he's not Junior," said Jessica. "He's the guy of my dreams, that's who he is. Watch this."

Jessica lowered her lashes and smiled for all she was worth. But the guy did not seem to notice the pretty twin sisters. Walking briskly, he crossed at the intersection and disappeared into the Bank Building on the other side of the street.

"Shoot." Jessica sighed. Then she brightened again. "Do you suppose he works around here, in the Bank Building or maybe even the Western Building? How old do you think he is? High school or college?"

"Let's see." Elizabeth pretended to give Jessica's questions thoughtful consideration. "He's a college sophomore named Tom. His major is economics, and he's on the baseball team. His favorite color is blue, and he likes Chinese food and horror movies."

"Very funny." Jessica glared at her twin. "This is serious."

"I know." Elizabeth looked at the computer printout and sighed. "It *is* serious. I haven't gotten any work done." She stuffed the printout back into her leather portfolio and jumped to her feet. "I'm going back inside."

With a last longing glance at the door through which the gorgeous guy had disappeared, Jessica gathered up her things. "I guess I will, too."

Walking toward the Western Building, Jessica and Elizabeth fell in behind two women who were talking in loud whispers. "I was going to do it at dinner last night," said the first woman, a platinum blonde. "I nerved myself up to tell him I was leaving him. But then he said he had a surprise for me. And guess what it was? He bought me a condo in Vail."

"A condo in Vail?" Her friend gasped. "I can't believe it, Maggie!"

Maggie? Jessica's ears pricked up.

"Believe it, Angela. A condo in Vail. Just because I casually mentioned the other day that I wanted to learn how to ski!"

"You can't leave him," Angela declared.

"That's what I thought," said Maggie. "So I called Craig and arranged a secret rendezvous after Frank went to bed. I tried to tell him it was over between us. But when he put his arms around me . . ."

The two women pushed through the revolving door. It was all Jessica could do to keep from dashing after them.

Jessica glanced at her twin. Elizabeth was staring after the women, her eyes bright with curiosity. "Aha!" Jessica proclaimed triumphantly. "I caught you. You're just as interested in Maggie as I am!"

Elizabeth smiled sheepishly. "I admit I was eavesdropping myself for a minute there."

"It's better than a soap opera," Jessica said as they entered the lobby. She craned her neck, but Maggie and Angela were gone. *No problem*, she thought. If she wanted to find out what had happened after Craig put his arms around Maggie, all she had to do was go upstairs and pick up her phone!

"Not more proofreading," Jessica groaned when she returned to her desk. "You'd think all anybody did around here was write."

Elizabeth laughed. "Gee, Jess. We must be working at a newspaper or something."

Still grumbling, Jessica sat down and began reading the article Katherine Francis, one of the reporters, had left for her. It was about upcoming events at the Sweet Valley Civic Center—and in Jessica's opinion was even more boring than Elizabeth's story on the library fundraiser. Pushing the pages away, Jessica picked up the telephone.

For a few seconds she heard only a dial tone. She replaced the receiver and tried again. "Home Shoppers Club," a man's voice announced.

Jessica smiled. What was that crazy lady going to buy now?

"I'd like to order the ginsu knife set, item number thirty-six," the woman requested. "Three of those, please. And item number nineteen, the spandex exercise outfit, size medium. I'd like four, one each in lime green, royal purple, bubblegum pink, and metallic silver."

"Not metallic silver," Jessica murmured. "No matter how you're shaped, it's bound to make you look like a station wagon!"

"What did you say?" Elizabeth asked, her eyes still on her work.

"Oh, nothing," Jessica replied quickly. "Just talking to myself."

The home shopping lady had almost finished her order when another line cut in. Jessica's eyes sparkled with anticipation. Would it be Maggie or Junior?

But these were voices she had not heard before. A man was talking to a young woman, and the conversation was short. "Coyote? It's Greenback," the man said.

"This is Coyote," the woman replied.

"Red fish up the coast highway to point seven," the man said next. "Delivery at ten o'clock. Got it?"

"Got it," the other caller confirmed.

There was a click, then a dial tone. Jessica replaced the receiver and wondered what the man had been talking about. Red fish up the coast highway? It sounded like some kind of a code!

Jessica shoved off from her desk and rolled her chair over to Elizabeth. "Liz, what do you think of this?" she asked excitedly. "A guy named Greenback was just talking to a girl named Coyote. And he said, 'Red fish up the coast highway to point seven. Delivery at ten o'clock.' What do you think that means?"

Elizabeth folded her arms across her chest and frowned at her twin. "Enough already, Jessica. You might find this sort of thing interesting, but I don't. I don't know what red fish up the coast highway means and I don't really care. I'm trying to get some work done!"

"Oh, come on, Liz," Jessica wheedled. "I bet it's a code. Help me figure out what it means. Red fish up the coast highway . . ."

"I doubt very much that it's a code. It was probably just someone from a shipping company or delivery service of some sort," Elizabeth suggested. "A truckload of seafood is now on its way to a restaurant up the coast."

"Oh." Jessica's face fell. That was a pretty logical explanation—and a pretty dull one. She rolled back to her own desk. "Well, sorry to bother you."

She picked up her receiver.

"You're not eavesdropping again, are you?" Elizabeth asked.

"For your information, Ms. Nosy, I'm placing a legitimate call to Amy to find out when the cookout starts tonight," Jessica said haughtily. "Mind your own business!"

But before she could dial, a man's voice came on the line. It was Greenback again! Jessica listened eagerly. "Rock? Greenback here. Cover drops at points three and seven. This time, cash up front from Hero."

The call ended and a dial tone returned. Jessica forgot that she had been planning to call Amy. Distracted, she contemplated these brief and mysterious messages. Greenback and Coyote, and now Rock and Hero. Who were these people with the wacky names?

Another voice gradually penetrated her consciousness. "Jessica. Jessica!"

Jessica snapped out of her trance. The receiver still pressed against her ear, she whirled in her chair to see Bill peering down at her quizzically.

"Oh, Bill, hi." Quickly, she hung up the phone. "What's up?"

"I wanted to look over that story Katherine gave you to proof," he said.

Jessica glanced at the article lying on her desk. She hadn't gotten past the headline. "Um . . . well . . . I'm not quite through with it."

"Jess." Bill pretended to frown at her, but there was a teasing sparkle in his bright blue eyes. "You seem to spend a lot of time gabbing on the phone. Making dates with all your boyfriends, right? Well, see if you can squeeze in a little proofreading somewhere."

Jessica grabbed her red pencil. "I'll get this right over to you," she promised.

Bill gave her shoulder a light pat. "Thanks, champ."

As Bill strode from the office Jessica saw her twin give her an I-knew-you'd-catch-it-one-of-these-days look. But Bill hadn't really been mad. Jessica could still feel his thrilling touch on her shoulder. It was a pretty good incentive to trade eavesdropping for proofreading . . . for a while, anyway.

I could really use a cup of coffee, Jessica thought. She yawned as she and Elizabeth pressed into the crowded elevator at the Western Building at nine A.M. on Wednesday. It was simply inhumane, having to get up so early in the morning during summer vacation!

But as the elevator shot upwards, Jessica's eyes snapped wide open. Standing right next to her was a woman wearing a poodle cardigan!

Jessica stepped on her sister's foot. "Ouch! Why'd you do that?" Elizabeth yelped.

Jessica nodded discreetly toward the poodle sweater. She had told Elizabeth all about the home shopping lady's many horrendous purchases. Now both girls put their hands to their mouths, trying to stifle their laughter. The lady in the poodle cardigan stared straight ahead.

Jessica thought she would explode. Finally, the elevator stopped at the fifth floor. The twins tumbled out into the hallway and through the door of the *News* office, giggles bursting from them. "Omigod, did you see that?" Jessica gasped. "It was even worse than I expected!"

"All those puffballs," Elizabeth agreed, wiping the tears of laughter from her eyes. "She *did* look exactly like a poodle!"

"And the worst thing is, she has five more of them at home!" They cracked up again.

"What's so funny, girls?" Rose asked.

"Oh, nothing," Jessica said. It was tempting to tell Rose about the home-shopping lady, but Elizabeth was the only person who knew about Jessica's crossed phone line, and Jessica didn't want it to get around the office that she was spending most of her time eavesdropping.

"Now I've discovered the identities of two of the people whose phone lines are crossed with mine," Jessica said to Elizabeth as they entered their office. "That only leaves Junior and Greenback. Maybe they work somewhere in the building, too!"

"Maybe so." Elizabeth grabbed a fresh yellow legal pad, then headed back for the door. "I'm going to find Anita. We're researching a story on the new Sweet Valley recycling program this morning. See you later."

Jessica contemplated the work that was waiting for her. She decided to start by transcribing the rest of a dictaphone tape Bill had given her the previous afternoon. Fifteen minutes later, she printed out her typing and trotted across the newsroom to the news editor's office. The door was closed. Pressing her ear to the door, Jessica heard a low mumble. Bill was on the phone. *I won't interrupt him*, she thought. *I'll just bring the typing by later.*

Jessica hurried back to her desk and picked up her telephone.

"Junior, are you listening?"

"Yes, Mother, I'm listening."

"If you keep spending your money faster than you earn it . . ."

As she eavesdropped on Junior and his mother, Jessica gazed idly out her window, which overlooked the street. The Bank Building was directly across from the Western Building, and from her own office on the fifth floor Jessica could look into its fifth-floor office. Suddenly she saw something that almost caused her to drop the phone. In the fifth-floor office of the Bank Building, as clear as day, she could see the guy of her dreams! The tall, blond, adorable guy she had spotted during lunch two days ago!

He was sitting on the edge of his desk, talking on the phone. The sun shining in his window glinted off his blond hair. His jacket was off and his sleeves were rolled up, and when he raised one wrist to check his watch Jessica could see that his arm was very muscular. Her heart pounded.

"He must have a summer job over there," she said breathlessly into the phone. "I bet he's a college student. I've just got to find a way to meet him!"

Junior's voice was abruptly replaced by a dial tone for a moment, and then another line crossed in. Jessica recognized Greenback's voice. As usual, he was giving delivery instructions to somebody—Rock, it sounded like. Jessica didn't pay much attention; she was too absorbed in the gorgeous vision across the street.

But then something in Greenback's voice made Jessica tune in to his conversation. "I've trusted you with a special job, Rock. She'll be at the usual place." Greenback's voice dropped to a rough, threatening whisper. "Make sure you take care of her, Rock. Don't disappoint me. Because if they don't find her body floating soon, they'll find *yours*."

Click. Greenback's voice was replaced by a dial tone.

The receiver fell from Jessica's hand onto the desktop with a clatter. She continued to stare out the window at the blond guy across the street, but she didn't really see him. She was completely stunned.

Exactly what had she overheard this time? Greenback's ominous words came back to her. *If they don't find her body floating . . .* Jessica shuddered, the blood in her veins suddenly feeling as cold as ice water. Had the two men on the phone been talking about *murder?*

Three

It couldn't be, Jessica thought, a worried frown creasing her forehead. *Of course not. I didn't just hear someone plotting a murder. I couldn't have!*

She realized her heart was racing and took a deep breath to calm herself. There had to be some other explanation. Hadn't she thought all along that Greenback and his friends were speaking in code? If so, then to talk about a body floating was probably code for something, too. It simply couldn't mean that somebody's body would be *literally* floating . . . that someone was to be drowned . . . murdered . . .

Jessica jumped up from her chair. She couldn't sit still thinking that somewhere in the building

Greenback, whoever he was, was planning a murder! It was just too creepy.

Elizabeth was not at her desk. Jessica dashed down the corridor to Anita's office. The door was ajar and the room empty. *That's right*, Jessica remembered. *Those two are off researching a story. They'll probably be out all day.*

Slowly, Jessica walked back to her own desk. She wanted very badly to tell someone about what she had just overheard, to get another opinion about what Greenback's words might mean. But at this point, no one except Elizabeth knew about Jessica's eavesdropping. Should she confide in one of the other interns?

Maybe I should call the police, Jessica thought, fidgeting with the gold lavaliere she wore on a delicate chain around her neck. Then she realized that would be pointless. She had no evidence to offer; all of Greenback's messages had been very brief and vague. She didn't know who he was; she wasn't even positive that the phone calls originated in the Western Building.

But if I continue to listen, I might hear more details! Quickly, Jessica picked up the telephone receiver. At that moment Bill strode into her office. "On the phone *again?*" he observed. "What's so interesting on that line?"

"Oh, I was just—"

"Come on, Jess." Bill stepped to her side and took her arm gently. "I've got a job that'll keep you busy. You're not going to like it, though," he added, a teasing note in his voice. "There's no phone in the room!"

Jessica spent the rest of the day in the newspaper morgue, a stuffy, windowless room lined with black file cabinets. Bill had deposited her there with an enormous box of what seemed to be about a million old newspaper articles and photographs. Jessica's job was to find the right place for each and every one. It was tempting just to stuff the articles and photographs randomly into the files, but she knew Bill would kill her if he caught her cheating.

Just when Jessica thought she could take no more, Bill came back and handed her a piece of paper. "Here's a list of some topics a few of the reporters are currently researching," he told her. "Hunt up whatever information you can find, OK?"

Jessica scanned the list. She was dying to get back to her crossed-line telephone, but with all this work she knew she never would. *Ugh. Why do people write about all these boring old topics? Why don't they write about recent things that can be called up from the computerized files?* Jessica wanted to scream.

She looked up at Bill. He smiled at her, and she melted. "Sure," she said. "No problem."

Several hours later, Jessica got to the last topic on the list. "George Fowler," she read out loud.

Somebody was writing an article about the new office tower being constructed next door. Well, there was bound to be a fat folder on Lila's high-profile father.

As Jessica pulled the Fowler file Elizabeth stuck her head in the room. "It's five o'clock, Jess," she announced. "Ready to go?"

"Am I ever!"

It was too late to eavesdrop any more that day, but at least now she could finally tell Elizabeth about what she had heard earlier. Jessica waited until they were in the parking garage before grasping her sister's arm. "Liz, I have to tell you what I heard on my phone today," she began urgently.

Elizabeth groaned. "Don't tell me. Let me guess. Maggie's husband got a hair transplant, so she decided to stick with him instead of running off with Craig. Or did the home-shopping lady finally reach the limit on her credit cards?"

"Nothing like that. It was something Greenback said. He was talking about some girl Rock was supposed to meet. And he said—" Jessica paused dramatically. " 'If they don't find her body floating soon, they'll find *yours*.' " Jessica faced her twin across the top of the Jeep, her expression intent. "Liz, I think they were planning to *kill* her!"

Elizabeth looked skeptical. "Kill her?" She fished in her purse for the keys to the Jeep.

"Don't you think you may be reading too much into it?"

"Well, then, what do *you* think they were talking about?" Jessica demanded.

"I have no idea," said Elizabeth. "Maybe they're not even real people. I mean, bodies floating and all that—it's so melodramatic. I bet you're picking up on a soap-opera hotline or something."

"They're real people," Jessica insisted. "It was Greenback, the same man I've heard a few times before. The one who *supposedly* runs a delivery service. It was a real conversation."

"All right," Elizabeth conceded as she started the engine and backed out of the parking space. "Still, I'm sure they weren't talking about a murder. They were probably just joking around."

"They weren't joking," Jessica cried. "You should have heard them, Liz. They were serious. Dead serious."

Elizabeth glanced at her twin. "This is really getting to you, isn't it?"

Jessica nodded.

"Well, I don't think you should worry." Elizabeth exited the parking garage and swung onto Main Street in the direction of home. "There's absolutely nothing you can do. I mean, let's say you *did* hear two real men talking about a real murder. You have no idea who the men are or who their prospective victim is, and you have no idea where the murder is supposed to take place!"

"I don't know who the men are," Jessica acknowledged. "But I'm pretty sure Greenback works in the building. I've got it! Tomorrow I'll check the directory in the lobby and see if there's a delivery service in the building!"

"If it'll make you feel any better, we can do that first thing in the morning," Elizabeth promised. "The point is, no matter what kind of strange things you've been overhearing, it's just incredibly unlikely that you've accidentally uncovered a murder plot unfolding in downtown Sweet Valley, of all places. I mean, really." She laughed. "Your imagination is running on overdrive. Maybe *you* should be the writer in the family!"

"I can't believe you're laughing at me," Jessica said.

"Oh, Jess. You know I'm on your side—I always am." Elizabeth stepped lightly on the gas as she left the business district behind. "I just think you shouldn't get so stressed out over this. Admit it: you don't have much to go on."

Jessica sighed. "You're right."

Elizabeth *was* right. But Jessica also knew she was not going to be able to get Greenback's latest message off her mind. All she could do was wait and hope she would have a chance to eavesdrop again the next day. Because one thing was for certain: Elizabeth might dismiss her fears as groundless, but Jessica had a very definite feeling that she hadn't heard the last of Greenback, Rock, and the floating body—not by a long shot.

"Any more murders in the works?" Elizabeth kidded her twin at the office the next morning.

Jessica hung up her phone and gave Elizabeth a dirty look. "No," she admitted reluctantly. "Greenback's made a few calls, but he just seems to be giving more shipping instructions. I guess it *is* just a delivery service after all." With a sigh, Jessica named a few of the companies listed in the Western Building directory that she and Elizabeth had decided were possible places of employment for Greenback. "Valley Transport Company. Mercury Messengers, Inc. Pacific Distribution . . ."

"Told you so," said Elizabeth. "But cheer up, Jess," she added wryly. "It's still early in the summer. You might meet a murderer yet."

Jessica nodded glumly. Then her eyes brightened. "First I'm going to meet *him*." Jessica pointed out the window to the office across the street.

Elizabeth followed her twin's gaze. "That's right," she said. "I'd almost forgotten about that guy."

"So did I. But what a mistake that would have been. Just look at him, Liz! He's perfect. Perfect for *me*," Jessica added, her eyes growing dreamy.

"I was wondering when you'd get your priorities straight," Elizabeth commented. "I've never seen you take so long to make a move on a boy who's caught your eye. It's been three whole days!"

"Well, I'm not going to waste any more time," Jessica decided. "I'm going to make sure we have a 'casual' encounter before the day's over. I'll devote my lunch hour to it."

"Speaking of which, it looks like he's on his way out," Elizabeth observed.

The cute guy had grabbed his jacket and was hurrying from his office. "That's my cue!" Jessica jumped up from her desk and dashed for the door. "Bye!"

"Hey, where's the fire?" a voice asked.

Elizabeth turned in her chair. Seth Miller was blocking her sister's path. "I'm glad I caught you," he said to Jessica. "I want to take you two out for lunch. What do you think about Chez Sam?"

Chez Sam was one of the poshest restaurants in Sweet Valley. But Elizabeth could see by Jessica's sour expression that she didn't feel like eating lunch anywhere with her sister and Seth. "I've got plans," Jessica said abruptly.

"No, she doesn't," Elizabeth told Seth. "We love Chez Sam!"

"Great." Seth beamed. "Well, let's go."

"Yeah, let's go!" Jessica urged. She sprinted to the elevator, Seth and Elizabeth at her heels.

Real smooth, Jess, Elizabeth thought as they hurried across the lobby. Jessica was hoping to get down to street level in time to bump into the cute guy. And they did reach the sidewalk just as he strode from his building. Elizabeth watched Jessica do everything to catch his attention but holler "Over here!" But he hurried off down the sidewalk without a single glance in their direction.

"It looks like he's got someplace important to go," Elizabeth remarked in a whisper.

Jessica frowned. "A lunch date," she surmised unhappily. "Probably with his girlfriend. After all, how could a hunk like that still be available?"

With the cute guy now just an unattainable speck in the distance, Jessica slowed down considerably. The three strolled at a leisurely pace to Chez Sam.

"I'm really excited about the series of articles we're going to be working on," Elizabeth said to Seth. "About retail and corporate growth in Sweet Valley." Elizabeth turned to Jessica. "This'll interest you, Jess. They're talking about expanding the Valley Mall! Tell her about it, Seth."

But Jessica barely paid attention as Seth described the negotiations now under way to build an addition to the mall. Elizabeth frowned. It wouldn't hurt if Jessica started taking her internship a little more seriously. Their boss, Bill, was on to the fact that Jessica spent most of her time on the telephone. Elizabeth would hate to see her twin get in trouble or, worse yet, fired. "Maybe Jessica could help us research this particular series of articles," she suggested.

"Sure, if Bill agrees," said Seth.

"Wouldn't that be fun, Jess?" Elizabeth asked.

Jessica looked blankly at her. "Hmm?"

Elizabeth shook her head. "Oh, forget it. We were just trying to come up with ways to make this internship more fun for you."

"Gee, thanks," Jessica replied.

Jessica's a hopeless case, Elizabeth decided as they entered the restaurant.

By the end of the lunch at Chez Sam, Jessica had regained her confidence. She had had plenty of time to consider the situation while Elizabeth and Seth engaged in an animated and entirely boring conversation about newspaper reporting and the latest mystery novel Seth had written in his spare time. *What difference does it make whether Mr. Gorgeous has a girlfriend or not?* Jessica thought, polishing off her plate of pasta primavera. *Once he lays eyes on me . . .*

"Do you think you'd ever quit journalism in order to write fiction full time?" Elizabeth asked Seth. "I mean, if you could make a living at it."

Jessica yawned. She wished they would gab a little less and eat a little more. They were never going to get out of the restaurant at this rate.

"Not a chance," Seth replied. "Writing mysteries is a kick. But it can't compare to reporting for the *News*. I love the excitement of working on a newspaper. I couldn't live without it."

"I love it, too," Elizabeth said. "This internship is so much fun! I'd be thrilled if I could land a job like yours when I get out of college. But I also want to keep up with my other writings, like my journal. There are some things I can say only there."

Jessica shifted in her chair. She was ready to scream when suddenly the check came. Seth opened his wallet and pulled out a few bills. Jessica couldn't help noticing that his wallet was stuffed with money.

He handed the check back to the waiter before Elizabeth could even peek at it. "This place is expensive, Seth," she said. "Let me and Jess pitch in a few dollars."

"Nope, it's on me," he insisted.

Jessica took her sister's wrist and turned it so she could see the time. One o'clock. She had better hurry if she wanted to catch the boy of her dreams on his way back to work.

"Thanks for lunch, Seth," Jessica said, jumping to her feet and tossing her napkin on the table. "I'll see you two back at the office."

"Jessica, where—"

Jessica didn't wait to hear the rest of

Elizabeth's question. Once outside she raced the four blocks back to the Bank Building. What luck! Coming right toward her from the opposite direction was Mr. Gorgeous.

Jessica paused to toss back her hair and smooth the front of her short linen dress. Then she strolled on in her very best traffic-stopping style.

Her timing was perfect. Her path was going to intersect his right in front of the Bank Building. *He must see me*, Jessica thought. *He's sure to stop.* And to make sure he did, she would use the oldest trick in the book.

Casually, Jessica let go of the strap of her pocketbook, letting it drop to the sidewalk. She waited for the cute boy to stop and pick it up for her. But he didn't even look her way. Brushing right past Jessica, a preoccupied expression on his finely chiseled face, he walked briskly into the Bank Building.

Jessica stood for a moment, her hands on her hips. What on earth was the matter with him? Was he *blind?*

She snatched up her pocketbook and stomped across the street to her own building. Then something occurred to her. For someone who had just had a lunch date with his girlfriend, Mr. Gorgeous didn't look too happy. Obviously there was trouble in paradise. Maybe they had even broken up!

Whatever the situation, Jessica was more determined than ever to meet this guy. She pushed through the revolving door of the Western Building, a smile blooming on her face. When it came to romance, she always liked a challenge. The harder someone was to catch, the more she wanted him!

Four

"That was pretty rude, bolting out of the restaurant like that when Seth had just treated you to a really nice, not to mention really expensive, lunch," said Elizabeth.

Elizabeth had returned to the office to find Jessica in her usual pose: sitting at her desk with the phone pressed against her ear and her eyes trained out the window at the office across the street.

"I thought maybe I'd run into Mr. Gorgeous," Jessica explained.

"Mr. Gorgeous, Greenback—they all sound like cartoon characters to me. Aren't you getting bored of spying and eavesdropping on people?"

Jessica hung up the phone with a sigh. She hated to admit it, but she *was* getting a little bored with the home-shopping lady and Maggie's endless soul-searching. And Greenback's delivery service had turned out to be a real disappointment. "Mr. Gorgeous is not a cartoon character," she told her twin. "And I'm not spying on him. Can I help it if his window's right across from mine?"

"I suppose not. Well, I'm off to the library to do some research." Notebook in hand, Elizabeth left the room.

Jessica stared out the window. Mr. Gorgeous was on the telephone again. And as he talked he looked out his window. *He's looking straight at me!* Jessica thought, sitting up eagerly.

Then she slumped again. No, his eyes were directed a little to the left. *The scenery's probably not nearly as good over there,* she wanted to inform him. When was he going to get a clue?

Out of habit, she picked up her phone and listened idly. Junior was calling the florist, ordering a big bouquet for his mother's birthday. *That's sweet,* Jessica thought. *His mom's a pain, but I guess he really loves her.*

Someone standing behind her cleared his throat and Jessica spun around in her chair, praying it wasn't Bill.

It was Bill. *How long has he been standing there?* she wondered, biting her lip. She really hoped he wasn't planning to hustle her off to the newspaper morgue again. She couldn't take being cooped up in there for another afternoon.

"You're not having problems with your phone, are you, Jessica?" he asked. "Rose says the whole system's a mess."

"Actually, I *am* having some trouble placing this call," Jessica lied. "I kept getting a wrong number, so now I'm waiting for the operator to assist me."

"Well, if you have any problems, tell Rose," Bill advised. "I just wanted to give you this." He handed her a dictaphone tape to transcribe. "No rush. And also, I wanted to let you know that I've volunteered your services to Bob Carlisle, the sports editor. He's covering the tennis invitational at the country club this weekend. I know you play tennis yourself, so I thought you might enjoy watching a few of the matches and helping Bob with the story."

Jessica lowered the receiver, her face lighting up in a pleased smile. "I'd love that. You know, you should come to the club yourself," she suggested. "It's going to be a great tournament."

"Unfortunately, I've got other plans this weekend."

"Hot date?" Jessica teased.

"A hot date with my laptop computer." Bill's lips curved in what Jessica thought was an incredibly sexy smile. "I'll be taking home a pile of work."

"You know what they say about all work and no play," Jessica warned.

"Oh, don't worry about me." Bill's smile deepened. "I've always known how to strike a balance. I'm still kind of new to this job, though. Still learning the ropes."

"I think you're a great news editor," Jessica gushed. "Were you a news editor before? At your old job in . . . where was it? New Orleans?"

"Denver. No, actually, my last job wasn't even at a newspaper," he replied. "Newspaper work is just one of the fields I've taken a shot at in the last few years."

"What else have you done?" Jessica asked.

"Oh, this and that," Bill said. "You could call me a jack of all trades." He cleared his throat again. "So, Jessica, don't forget to check in with Bob at some point today or tomorrow. I hope it'll be fun for you to cover the tournament. I want to keep my interns happy."

"Oh, I'm happy," Jessica assured him.

Bill winked at her, then disappeared. Jessica heaved a sigh and spun her chair around in a circle. *It should be illegal to be that good-looking*, she thought, picturing Bill's smile and the twinkle in his eyes. Too bad she couldn't work with *him* on a special assignment instead of with boring old Bob. Meanwhile, she still didn't know for sure that Bill had a girlfriend. *He has to, though*, she figured. *Probably three or four!*

Jessica looked out the window. The blond boy was still on the phone—and still adorable. "Don't worry," she whispered. "I haven't forgotten about you!"

Checking her in box, Jessica found some copy-editing work from Katherine. She picked up her pencil and began reading the printout. Then with her free hand she reached for the phone. There was no reason why she shouldn't listen in on the other lines while she was editing, she decided. It would be good background noise, kind of like having the radio on.

Cradling the receiver between ear and shoulder, Jessica made a few marks on the page. Maggie was telling her friend Kim about a recent secret rendezvous with Craig.

"We met at the country club, as usual," Maggie began.

The country club . . . hmm, Jessica thought. *Maybe Craig's a tennis or golf pro. Maybe I'll get a look at him this weekend!*

"And he asked me to run away with him right then and there. Kim, he got down on his knees and begged me. I've never had a man want me that much!"

Wow, thought Jessica. *Neither have I!*

"He told me I was breaking his heart," Maggie continued. "Stringing him on like this. And I told him he had to understand that—Kim, I'll have to call you back. My next appointment is here."

Maggie and Kim hung up. For a moment

there was a dial tone. Jessica pushed the button on the phone and a familiar man's voice cut in. It was Greenback, talking to Rock. Jessica was about to hang up; the delivery messages were so routine at this point. But Rock's next words stopped her.

"It's done," Rock said to Greenback. "I got all ten packets off her, too."

Packets? Jessica wondered.

"Ten? There should have been more than that." Greenback's voice became grim. "I knew she was holding out on us. It serves her right," he snarled.

The phone went dead.

A chill ran down Jessica's spine. She clutched the receiver, her fingers suddenly frozen with fear. Were Rock and Greenback talking about the same girl they had been discussing the other day, the day of the floating body conversation? *It's done . . . It serves her right . . .* Did that mean what Jessica thought it did?

If it did, then Elizabeth had been wrong after all, and Jessica's original suspicion was right. And if that was the case, then it was too late to do anything about it.

Jessica squeezed her eyes shut, wishing she could erase from her memory the conversation she had just heard. *It's done,* Rock had said. Well, he could have been talking about anything, she rationalized. They were mad at the girl for some reason, because of the packets.

Maybe Rock had just talked to her and threatened her. Jessica desperately wanted to believe that.

Suddenly, her phone rang, sounding shrill and insistent in the quiet office.

Jessica's heart jumped into her throat. She was afraid to pick it up. What if it was a man's voice on the other end? Greenback—or Rock, the murderer?

Her hand trembling, Jessica gingerly lifted the receiver. "H-hello?" she stuttered.

"Hi, Jess. It's Lila."

Jessica had never been so glad to hear her friend's voice. She exhaled in a huge sigh of relief. "Lila, hi. What's up?"

"Surf's up," Lila replied. "It's an absolutely perfect beach day and I've noticed lately that your tan could use some work. Can you get away from the office?"

Jessica hesitated. "I don't think so, Li. It's only one-thirty. I have a bunch of stuff to do."

"Oh, can't it wait?"

"Well . . ." Jessica considered. There were a few things in her in box, but none was marked urgent. And Bill had said there was no rush on the typing.

"You could always go back to the office later this afternoon," Lila pointed out.

"I don't have a bathing suit or anything with me," Jessica said.

"You can borrow one of mine," offered Lila. "I'll bring a towel for you, too."

There was really no reason not to go, Jessica decided. And now that she thought about it, she realized she would love to get away from the Western Building for a while . . . and leave her deadly crossed phone line far behind.

"OK," she agreed. "I'm up for it."

"Great. I'll meet you at the usual place," Lila said.

"No, somebody might see me there. And if anyone asks, I'm going to have to say I was doing errands for one of the reporters this afternoon," said Jessica. "Let's try Castle Cove."

"Fine. See you in half an hour!"

Jessica was a bundle of nerves as she hung up and began to write a note for Elizabeth. *I took the Jeep—doing some research out of the office—can you get a ride home from Seth?* she scribbled. Then she stuck the note in an envelope so no one else would read it and hurried from the newsroom, glad that Rose was momentarily distracted.

As she pointed the Jeep out of town and headed north up the coast highway, Jessica slowly felt her tension melt away. The sun was shining, and a mild ocean breeze stirred her hair and caressed her skin. She didn't know what Greenback and Rock had been talking about, but she decided that it just *couldn't* be murder. On such a beautiful day, it was simply impossible to believe that anything so dire could be happening in Sweet Valley.

Castle Cove was a secluded, white-sand beach surrounded by tall cliffs. Jessica didn't go there that often—there was a beautiful beach right in Sweet Valley—but she loved it when she did. A lot of college students and artistic types hung out there; it was a sophisticated scene.

She parked the Jeep. Lila, wearing dark sunglasses and an oversized T-shirt, waved to her from the other side of the parking lot.

"Here," Lila said when Jessica had joined her. She handed Jessica her beach bag. "The suit's in there."

Jessica peeked into the beach bag. "Which one did you bring me?" She pulled out a plain red bikini. "Lila, this is your oldest suit. I can't believe you brought me this old rag!"

"Look, Jess, you may be my best friend, but that doesn't mean I'm about to loan you one of my brand-new bikinis."

"You're just trying to make sure you'll look better than me," Jessica accused.

Lila smiled smugly. "Shut up and change so we can start scoping. This place is crawling with fantastic-looking guys!"

A few minutes later, Jessica emerged from the changing room. She and Lila strolled across the sand, searching for the perfect vantage point. "How about here?" Jessica suggested.

Lila spread out her striped beach towel. Removing their coverups, the two girls sat down and began applying suntan lotion to their arms and legs.

"Aren't you going to thank me?" Lila wanted to know.

"Thank you for what? Loaning me your crummiest bathing suit?"

"No, for rescuing you from the stuffy, ultra-dull newspaper office." Lila adjusted the top of her strapless black bikini. "Admit it. This is the life."

Jessica gazed around her. The Pacific Ocean sparkled like a gem; the sky was just as brilliantly blue as the water below it. And two incredibly cute college guys were walking along the water's edge, right toward them!

Jessica wriggled her bare toes in the warm, soft sand. "Yep. This is the life."

"Don't you just wish you were me?" Lila said airily. She tilted her face to the sun, tossing back her long, glossy brown hair. "I can hang out at the beach every single day."

Jessica scowled. She *had* wished, on more than one occasion, that she was Lila. Or rather, that she was as rich as Lila, but there was no reason to let Lila know this. "I *like* my summer job," she lied. "I'm learning a lot. And the reporters are all really handsome—as handsome as these guys." She nodded at the college boys.

Lila lowered her glasses to make an inspection. "Yeah, but the reporters don't strut around the office in their shorts."

Jessica laughed. "You've got a point there!"

The two boys cast appreciative glances in their direction. Jessica and Lila smiled invitingly. But before the guys could make a move, their arms were grabbed by two girls and they were dragged back down the beach.

Jessica sighed, thinking of Bill and Mr. Gorgeous. "The really cute ones always seem to be taken."

"Don't give up so easily," counseled Lila. "Check out the action over there."

In the other direction, a bunch of tanned, well-muscled boys in bright swim trunks were setting up a volleyball net. "I'll give them four minutes," Lila said, glancing at her gold wristwatch.

"Four minutes for what?"

"Four minutes until they come over here to ask us if we want to play," Lila explained.

"You're on." Jessica smiled. "I think it'll take five."

She lay back on her towel and idly sifted sand through her fingers. The warm sun was so relaxing! *I never want to go back to the office again*, Jessica thought. If she never went back, she would never be tempted to eavesdrop. And if she never eavesdropped, she would never again have to listen to Greenback and Rock's creepy voices and disturbing, mysterious messages.

"Do you *really* like being an intern at the *News?*" Lila asked, as if she didn't believe such a thing could be possible.

"Yeah—sort of," Jessica responded. "I mean, some of it is pretty boring, like the typing and filing. But the people are cool, for the most part."

Jessica turned her head to study Lila's pretty profile. Why not tell Lila about the conversations she had been overhearing on the crossed phone lines—and especially about the latest, scary one? It would be a relief to share it with someone. *Lila's bound to laugh it off,* Jessica anticipated. *And then I'll be able to laugh it off, too.*

"There's one really weird thing, though," Jessica began.

And then they heard a blood-curdling scream from the other end of the beach, where the tall, rocky cliffs came in close to the water's edge.

Jessica and Lila sat up abruptly. Lifting their hands to shade their eyes from the sun, they stared down the beach. Jessica saw people running and shouting. A crowd had gathered.

"What a commotion!" Lila cried. She sprang to her feet. "Come on, Jess. Let's go see what it's about!"

Suddenly a wave of terror overcame Jessica, and her whole body stiffened. She sat frozen, unable to rise.

"Snap out of it, Jess," Lila urged, gripping her friend's arm. "What's the matter, do you have sunstroke or something?"

Lila hauled Jessica to her feet and gave her a shove to get her started. Jessica trotted along at Lila's side, but she barely felt the sand under her feet. It was as if she had no control over her own limbs. A vague, inexplicable dread had numbed her from head to toe.

The words she had overheard on the telephone earlier that afternoon started repeating in her brain. *It's done . . . it's done . . . serves her right . . . serves her right . . .*

Lila and Jessica neared the group of people. There was a buzz of raised voices; a few people were crying hysterically. "The police! Somebody call the police!" a man shouted urgently.

Lila pressed forward, curious to see the object on the sand. Jessica hung back. She wanted only to press her hands against her eyes. She didn't want to see.

But just then, the crowd of milling, excited people parted momentarily. Jessica caught a quick glimpse of what everyone was staring at. And a glimpse was all she needed. A bedraggled bundle of dripping clothing, a swirl of wet hair, the bloated, corpse-pale skin . . . it was a woman's body, just as Jessica had known it would be.

Lila gasped. "It's a dead body! Somebody drowned!" she cried.

Jessica felt herself choking. She tried to suck in a breath of air, but she couldn't. Her throat had closed up. She felt herself growing dizzy. The sea and the sky started spinning around her. She put out a hand, reaching for Lila. But before Jessica could clasp her friend's arm, blackness swamped her and she tumbled backward onto the sand.

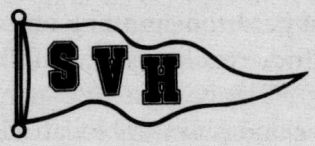

Five

"Are you sure you don't want any dinner, honey?" Alice Wakefield asked her daughter that evening at home.

Jessica shook her head. "No, thanks, Mom," she said, her voice thin and small. "It smells great. But I'm—I'm just not hungry."

The rest of the family, including her older brother, Steven, and his college friend Adam Maitland, was having dinner in the kitchen. Both boys were prelaw students and had summer jobs with local law firms. But Jessica hadn't been able to bring herself to join them. Instead, she sat huddled on the den couch, a crocheted afghan wrapped around her shoulders. She had had two cups of hot herbal tea, but she was still shivering.

Why do I feel so cold? she wondered. *I feel as cold as a body that's been floating in the icy ocean . . . a dead body.*

Mrs. Wakefield touched her wrist to Jessica's forehead. "I'm worried about you. But you don't have a fever."

"I'm just shaken up. I'll be all right," Jessica promised. "I'll eat something later."

Her mother bent to give her a kiss. "Let me know if you want anything."

Mrs. Wakefield returned to the kitchen. A minute later, Elizabeth appeared, carrying a plate. "Can I eat my dinner in here with you?" she asked her twin.

Jessica nodded. "Sure."

"Do you want the TV on?" Elizabeth picked up the remote control. "It's so quiet in here."

Jessica shrugged, pulling the afghan closer around her. "Whatever."

Elizabeth hit the on button. "The body of an unidentified teenaged girl was found at Castle Cove Beach this afternoon," the TV news anchorman announced. "The cause of death has not yet—"

"Turn it off!" Jessica cried, a sharp sob escaping her.

Quickly, Elizabeth switched off the television. "Sorry about that." She put her arm around Jessica's shoulders and hugged her. "It must have been scary being on the beach when they found the body."

"It was more than scary." Jessica sniffled. "I heard those men planning to murder her. I feel like *I* helped kill her!"

"You didn't help kill anyone." Elizabeth gave her twin a gentle shake. "You can't be sure exactly what you heard. And they haven't said *anything* about the girl being murdered. She drowned. It happens. People swim out too far—"

"She was fully clothed," Jessica said dully. "She hadn't been out for a swim."

"Then it could have been a boating accident," Elizabeth said. "She could even have committed suicide. It's a terrible thing, Jess. But don't make yourself feel more terrible by imagining something that's just not true."

"You don't know that." Jessica looked at Elizabeth. "You can't say for sure that she wasn't murdered. You didn't see her lying there." Her voice dropped to a shaky whisper. "You didn't hear those men's voices. You can't say for sure."

"No," Elizabeth finally admitted reluctantly. Doubt and uncertainty clouded her blue-green eyes. "I can't say for sure."

"Good, you're finally here," Seth greeted Elizabeth on Friday morning. "Come on. We've got a story to cover."

"Finally here?" Elizabeth looked at her watch. "It's only eight-forty-five. I'm not late, I'm early."

"Well, the news won't wait." Seth steered her

back toward the elevator. Then he glanced around. "Hey, where's Jessica? Bill assigned the story to us, but I'm sure he wouldn't mind if she tagged along. There's going to be a press conference at the police station. Do you think she'd want to come with us to find out the latest on the drowning victim?"

Elizabeth grimaced. That was the last thing Jessica would want to do! But she didn't say this to Seth. Jessica had made Elizabeth promise not to tell anyone at the newspaper that she had been at Castle Cove the previous afternoon. She was afraid of getting in trouble for playing hooky. "She's not here yet," Elizabeth said. "She overslept. My mom's going to bring her by later this morning."

"Too bad," said Seth. "She's been looking bored lately, like she could use a little drama in her life."

"Hmm," Elizabeth murmured. *A little drama. What an understatement!*

Jingling his keys, Seth led Elizabeth down aisle C of the seventh level of the parking garage. He stopped next to a brand-new black Mazda RX-7.

Elizabeth looked around for his red Celica. "Where's your car?" she asked.

"Right here." Seth patted the hood of the Mazda. "What do you think? I picked it up yesterday after work."

"It's beautiful," Elizabeth breathed. "I didn't know you were planning to buy a new car!"

"It was kind of an impulse purchase," Seth admitted.

"Wow. That was some impulse."

Seth unlocked the door on the passenger side. "Hop in. I don't know much about the accident," he told Elizabeth as they sped to the Sweet Valley police station. "No more than what you and everybody else in Sweet Valley know at this point. A young woman's body was found washed up at Castle Cove yesterday afternoon, presumably drowned. The police weren't releasing a lot of information last night, probably because they didn't have all that much. But there may be some new developments this morning. They're briefing the press at nine."

"I wonder who she was," Elizabeth mused. "I wonder how she died."

"That's what we're going to find out."

At the station, they crowded into a conference room with a number of other reporters from local newspapers and TV and radio stations. Seth and Elizabeth prepared to take notes.

Sergeant Jack Wilson, a twenty-five-year veteran on the Sweet Valley police force, began the briefing at nine o'clock sharp and without preamble. "We have not yet identified the young woman whose body was found yesterday at Castle Cove. She doesn't appear to be a local resident, however. No missing-person reports have been filed in this area during the last few months."

"Probably a runaway," Seth whispered in Elizabeth's ear. "It could be weeks before they can identify her."

"But one thing is now definite." Sergeant Wilson paused. Something about his somber expression made Elizabeth sit forward on her chair and hold her breath. "The young woman did not drown accidentally. According to the autopsy conducted at the hospital late last night, she was strangled to death before she went into the water."

Elizabeth gasped. *Strangled!*

Throughout the conference room, there was a hum of excited voices. Pens and pencils flew as the reporters jotted down Sergeant Wilson's surprising words.

"That's all," Sergeant Wilson concluded. "We'll keep you posted as we learn more about the case. And as always, if you come up with any leads that would help further the investigation . . ."

Seth was already on his feet. Elizabeth dashed after him. "Let's get back to the office," he said. "It looks like this is going to be a much bigger story than I expected!"

The staff of the *Sweet Valley News* listened quietly as Seth filled them in on what he and Elizabeth had learned so far. Shock and excitement registered on everyone's face. A violent murder had taken place, right there in the Sweet Valley area. This kind of story was rare.

"I'll begin my investigation into the girl's identity immediately, and Liz will assist me," Seth announced. "Rose, we'll probably be out of the office all day. Any calls that come in about the story—"

"You can pass them along to me," Bill directed. "I'll field them."

Elizabeth and Seth's colleagues pressed forward, eager to ask more questions. Elizabeth noticed that only one person hung back, silent and pale.

Leaving Seth to discuss the case with the others, Elizabeth crossed the newsroom to her sister's side. "Jessica, are you feeling OK?"

"Liz, we have to talk." Seizing Elizabeth's arm, Jessica pulled her through the nearest door and into the newspaper's library. She shut the door behind them. Before speaking, she peered around the room, making sure that she and Elizabeth were its only occupants.

"Liz, I knew that girl had been murdered," Jessica said in a low, urgent voice. "I knew even before you heard it from the police!"

"You were right about that," Elizabeth acknowledged. "But that still doesn't mean that there's a connection between—"

"There *is* a connection," Jessica insisted. Elizabeth didn't know when she had ever seen her usually lighthearted twin so serious. "There just has to be. Right after lunch yesterday, I heard those two men talking. 'It's done,' Rock said." Jessica hugged herself, as if she felt a sudden chill. "And later that afternoon there was the dead body, floating just the way they'd said it would be. There *is* a connection," she repeated firmly. "Liz, I heard the murder being arranged. I heard the murderers' voices. And one of those men—Greenback, the one who makes all the phone calls—he's probably here in Sweet Valley. I bet he's right here in the Western Building!"

Jessica's words were like icy fingers on Elizabeth's skin. She shivered. "It—it could be a coincidence," she reminded her twin.

"Do you really believe that?"

Elizabeth was silent for a moment. Jessica's fear that there was a link between her eavesdropping and the murdered girl was contagious.

But common sense told Elizabeth that much more evidence was needed before a conclusion could be reached. "I don't know *what* I believe," she told Jessica. "I guess I'm still not one hundred percent convinced that there's any significance to the phone calls you overheard."

"Well, I'm one hundred and *ten* percent convinced," Jessica declared. "Liz, I've got to do something. I can't keep this to myself any longer."

Elizabeth nodded. "It's time to go to the police and tell them what you know," she encouraged her sister. "It might not be helpful—the calls might not be related to the crime. But then again, they could be a real clue!"

At noon, Jessica slung her purse over her shoulder and walked purposefully out of the newspaper office to the elevator. She hoped her nervousness didn't show; she didn't want any of her co-workers asking her if anything was wrong.

If only Liz were here! Jessica wished. She would have liked her twin's support on this errand.

The elevator door slid open. A man in a business suit and wire-rimmed glasses stood inside, reading a newspaper. Frozen, Jessica stared at him.

He looked up at her. "Are you heading down?" he asked.

Jessica shook her head. "No, I—go ahead."

The elevator door closed. Jessica realized her heart was pounding like a drum. No, she decided, heading for the stairs. There was no way she was going to take the elevator and risk getting trapped in it with Greenback or one of his murderous partners.

As soon as she was in the Jeep, Jessica locked the doors and sighed in relief. She couldn't wait to get to the police station and finally tell her story to the authorities!

At the station, she marched right up to the officer at the reception desk. "Can I help you?" he asked.

Jessica peered at the name tag on his uniform. "Yes, Officer Inman. I'm here to give you some information about the murdered girl on the beach!"

Officer Inman raised his eyebrows. "What kind of information?"

"Well, it's kind of a long story," Jessica explained. "There's this phone problem at my office—the lines are all mixed up because of some construction next door. So I keep hearing other people's conversations on my extension. First I heard a woman talking to her friends about cheating on her husband. Then there's this woman who calls the Home Shoppers Club all the time. You wouldn't believe the junk she buys! But the really interesting conversations, the ones that relate to your case, are between this man, Greenback, and a bunch of other people. Usually he just gives them instructions for deliveries of some sort. But the other day—Wednesday—he said something to a man about a floating body, and then yesterday the other man told him it was done. It was *done!*" Jessica repeated. "The *murder* was done. That's what they were talking about!"

Officer Inman's expression, at first interested, now seemed skeptical. *He thinks I'm a total flake,* Jessica realized dejectedly. *Why did I go on and on about the Home Shoppers Club? I should've gotten right to the good stuff!*

"Your information may be of some use to the

officers investigating the case," he said politely. "I'll send you along to Detective Jason. Three doors down on the right."

Obediently, Jessica walked down the hall and knocked on Detective Jason's door. "Come in," he called.

Jessica entered, feeling less confident than she had even a minute earlier. "Officer Inman sent me. I thought I might know something about the murder case, but maybe—"

"He just buzzed me about you. Sit down."

Jessica sat down. To her relief, Detective Jason looked at her with pronounced interest. "I'm intrigued," he began. "Officer Inman said you've been overhearing something on your office telephone that you believe may be related to the murder case. Where do you work?"

"I work at the *Sweet Valley News*," Jessica said. "On the fifth floor of the Western Building. The phone system has been messed up for weeks because of the Fowler Tower construction, and for some reason my line is crossed with a bunch of others. Sometimes instead of a dial tone I hear voices."

"The *News*, eh?" Detective Jason jotted something on a piece of paper. "How long have you worked there, Ms. . . . ?"

"Wakefield," she said. "Jessica Wakefield. I'm just a summer intern."

"OK, Ms. Wakefield. Tell me exactly what you've overheard. Stick to the calls that you feel are connected to the case. Take your time and be precise."

Jessica told Detective Jason about Greenback and the delivery-service calls to people with names like Rock, Coyote, Hero, and Chopper. She was thrilled to see the detective writing down her every word. There was nothing she liked better than a captive audience!

"I thought those calls were pretty mysterious," Jessica continued, remembering how poor, unimaginative Elizabeth had dismissed her intuitions regarding them. "But until two days ago, I didn't think they were dangerous. That was when I heard Greenback order Rock to kill someone. A girl."

Detective Jason lifted his eyebrows; Jessica was glad to see he looked impressed by this startling development in her narrative. "Did he say that in so many words?" he asked.

"No," she admitted. "He said, 'If they don't find her body floating, they'll find *yours* soon,' or something like that." She wrinkled her nose. "I guess that's kind of vague, but—"

"It's not at all vague," Detective Jason declared. "I think you were entirely right to find it highly suspicious, Ms. Wakefield."

Jessica sat up straighter in her chair. "It *was* highly suspicious," she agreed. "Especially in light of the conversation I overheard yesterday . . . the day of the murder."

She paused for dramatic effect. Detective Jason

appeared to be hanging on her every word. "What did you hear?" he asked, pencil poised.

"Rock informed Greenback that *it* was *done*. They talked about some packets that Rock had gotten from the girl. And then Greenback said that she'd been holding out on them and so it served her right."

Detective Jason whistled. "I really think you might have something here, Ms. Wakefield. I'm very glad you came to us with this. If it turns out that these delivery-service messages are related to the case, and I have a hunch they are, they just may lead us to the killer!"

Jessica beamed. "I'm happy to help in any way I can," she assured him.

"You've already been a big help. Now, let me get a little more information from you, for the record."

Detective Jason asked her a number of questions about her job at the *News* and her fellow employees. Then he wrote down her phone numbers at home and work and her home address.

When he was done, he tapped his pencil and studied Jessica. "Who else knows about the calls you've overheard?"

"Only my twin sister, Elizabeth," answered Jessica. "And she didn't really believe me when I told her they might be linked to this murder."

"Hmm." Detective Jason put down his pencil. "I think that'll do for now."

"So what should I do?" Jessica asked.

"Keep listening to your phone," he instructed. "Tell me absolutely everything you overhear. Once we figure out the code, the delivery-service messages may provide us with invaluable clues."

Jessica hopped to her feet. Suddenly, the murder case didn't seem so scary to her—it just seemed exciting. She couldn't wait to get back to the office and tell everyone about the important role she was going to play in the police investigation!

"One other thing, and this is very important, Ms. Wakefield." Detective Jason crossed the office and placed a hand on her arm. "You need to be very discreet. From now on, don't talk about this with anybody else—at the office, or even here at the station. Not even your sister. I must be your sole contact. We can't risk a leak. We don't want Greenback to know you're on to him."

Jessica shivered. She sure *didn't* want that!

"It's in the interest of cracking this difficult and dangerous case, Ms. Wakefield," Detective Jason reiterated. "And it's for your own safety."

She nodded. She was a little disappointed, though, that she couldn't broadcast the fact that she was playing detective for the Sweet Valley police.

"I won't tell anyone," Jessica vowed. *Except Elizabeth and the rest of my family*, she added silently.

"Good." Detective Jason squeezed her arm. "We'll keep in touch."

Feeling very important, Jessica bounded out of the station. She cast a pitying glance at Officer Inman as she went. *Poor guy,* she thought. *He obviously wouldn't see a clue if it hit him in the eye!*

Six

"How was the tennis tournament?" Elizabeth asked when Jessica returned from the country club late Saturday afternoon.

Elizabeth, Steven, and Adam were lounging by the pool in the backyard, drinking tall glasses of iced tea and munching nachos.

Jessica helped herself to a tortilla chip dripping with cheese. "I saw a couple of dynamite matches," she replied. "The finals are tomorrow, but of course Bob gets to cover those. Still, he said he'd incorporate my notes into his article for Monday's paper. You guys'll have to help me come up with some good action words for my write-up."

"Next you'll be getting your own byline in the

paper," said Adam. "Jessica Wakefield, cub reporter!"

"Oh, that's nothing," Jessica drawled. "When I help crack this murder case, my name *and* my picture will be plastered all over the *News*."

Her father stepped out onto the patio in time to hear Jessica's last words. "I hope you haven't been talking like that at the country club," he said. "Remember Detective Jason's advice about being discreet."

"I'm being very discreet," Jessica assured him. "I've only told you guys. None of *you* is in league with Greenback, are you?" she joked.

"Seriously, Jess." Mr. Wakefield shook some charcoal onto the grill. "Your mother and I would feel much better about your participating in the police investigation if we knew you were doing just as Detective Jason said."

"I am, Daddy." Jessica ran over to give her father a hug. "I'm just relieved, that's all. I feel so much safer since I went to the police!"

"That's just the way it should be," Mr. Wakefield observed before heading back into the house.

"By the way, did I get any phone calls?" Jessica asked, returning to the plate of nachos for another chip.

"Amy and Lila both called," Elizabeth told her.

"And there were a bunch of hang-up phone calls," Steven added.

Jessica frowned. "Hang-up phone calls?"

"Yeah. You know, the kind where you pick up the phone and the person on the other end hangs up without saying anything."

"Probably wrong numbers," Jessica hypothesized.

"My theory is it's some guy trying to get up his nerve to ask one of you two out," Steven said. He turned to Adam. "You wouldn't believe how many guys call this house. It's absurd."

"The only guy who calls me is Todd," Elizabeth interjected.

"Well, plenty of guys call *me*," Jessica acknowledged, dimpling for Adam's benefit. "And I'm not ashamed to say so!"

As if on cue, the phone rang. Steven picked up the portable phone and pulled out the antenna. "Hello?"

He looked at Jessica. Covering the mouthpiece, he hissed, "This time he got up the courage to ask for you. Go easy on the poor guy!"

Jessica took the phone. "Hello?" she said, her tone neutral. She didn't want to sound *too* inviting; it could be some loser.

There was no answer on the other end of the line. But the person didn't hang up, either. Jessica could hear him breathing. "Hello?" she repeated, a tight knot suddenly forming in her stomach. "Who is this?"

There was no reply. Quickly, Jessica slammed the antenna back down. Her hand shaking, she handed the phone back to her brother.

"I guess he chickened out after all," Steven observed.

"Yeah." Jessica's voice was barely audible. "I guess so."

Elizabeth frowned. "What's wrong, Jess? Was it an obscene phone call?"

Jessica shook her head. "He didn't say anything." She sat down on the edge of the one of the lounge chairs. "I just feel like . . . it's like someone's checking up on me."

"That's impossible," Steven said. "This Greenback person isn't eavesdropping on you, *you're* eavesdropping on *him*. He doesn't know anyone's listening to him. And even if he did, he'd have no way of knowing it was you. You couldn't be more anonymous."

Jessica smiled. Her brother was going to make a good lawyer someday, she thought. He was so logical.

"Steven's right," Elizabeth agreed. "It's probably just some guy from school who has a crush on you. Don't worry, Jess."

"OK. I won't," she said. But as she sank back in the lounge chair, she wasn't at all sure she could keep from worrying. Her family was being logical, but logic didn't have anything to do with the feeling Jessica had deep in her gut. She would have bet anything that the caller wasn't a high school boy with a crush. The caller had something to do with Greenback . . . and the murder.

"I wish you could stick around the office this morning," Jessica said to Elizabeth on Monday. "Can't Seth go by himself to investigate the murder story?"

"He really needs my help," Elizabeth replied. "Besides, this is the biggest story of the summer—maybe of the year. I want to be in on it!"

"You can be in on it right here," Jessica pointed out. "Help me eavesdrop on Greenback!"

Elizabeth gathered together her notebook and folders. "You'll be fine on your own, Jess. The newspaper office is the safest place in the world to be. I bet we'll be back by lunchtime. I'll see you then."

It was an uneventful morning. Jessica copy-edited a few stories and transcribed a dictaphone tape for Bill. In between, she listened on her phone. She heard the latest installment in the Maggie-Frank-Craig love triangle, but there wasn't a single delivery-service call.

At twelve, Elizabeth still had not returned. There was no point waiting for her, Jessica figured. She and Seth were probably hot on the trail of their story, and lunch would be the furthest thing from their minds. Jessica didn't really feel like eating with any of the other interns. She was a bit on edge, and she didn't want anybody asking why. *I'll just run to the coffee shop and grab a sandwich*, she decided.

At the elevator, Jessica pressed the down button. When the door opened, she couldn't help smiling. The poodle cardigan lady was inside! Today she was wearing a gaudy necklace of king size pearls. Jessica resisted the urge to lean over and whisper, "I know those are fake!"

The home–shopping lady got off on the second floor, leaving Jessica momentarily alone with the elevator's one other occupant. She stole a look at him out of the corner of her eye. He was less corporate-looking than most of the people who worked in the Western Building. His blond hair was long and he was wearing a baseball cap and dark glasses. He didn't pay any attention to Jessica; still, she was glad she had only one more floor to go.

On the main floor, Jessica walked briskly across the lobby to the coffee shop. She paid for a chef's salad and a bottle of apple juice, then chose a small table by the door. She picked up her fork and was about to dig into the salad when she noticed someone sitting down at the next table. It was a man in a baseball cap and sunglasses. The man from the elevator!

Is he following me? Jessica wondered, her heart skipping a beat. He certainly looked suspicious. He was just sitting there; he hadn't purchased anything to eat or drink. *Maybe he's waiting to meet someone,* she thought. *Then again, maybe he's waiting for me to leave so he can follow me and attack me in the elevator or the stairwell!*

Jessica poked nervously at her salad. *I'm just imagining things,* she told herself. Hadn't Steven reminded her that there was no way the murderer could be on to her eavesdropping, much less know her identity? Even so, she had lost her appetite. Trying to look unconcerned, Jessica took a bite of the salad, but she could barely chew and swallow it. Her nerves were too strained.

As casually as she could, Jessica glanced at the man in the baseball cap. He was staring straight at her! At least, it looked as if he was; Jessica couldn't see his eyes behind the dark glasses.

Leaving her salad unfinished, she sprang to her feet and raced from the coffee shop. As she ran into the lobby she plowed into a man walking across her path.

The man grabbed her arm and Jessica yelped with fright. She was about to hit him with her purse when she looked up into his face. It was the cute guy from across the street!

In all the excitement over the murder case, Jessica hadn't had time to work on her plan to meet him. Now here they were—and he'd practically taken her in his arms. Instantaneously, Jessica's fear was transformed into delight. Collecting herself, she hurried to make the most of this lucky accident. "I am *so* sorry," she apologized. Instead of stepping back from him, she remained close, holding his gaze. "Don't I know you from somewhere?"

It wasn't the most original line, but it was the best she could come up with on such short notice. And Jessica figured he would be glad for any opener she gave him. Besides, maybe he would recognize her, too, now that they were finally face to face. She was pretty sure she had seen him looking across the street in her direction on a few occasions.

But he just shook his head. "I don't think so," he muttered distractedly. "Excuse me." He stepped around her and hurried across the lobby and out of the building, leaving Jessica staring after him, her hands on her hips.

After making sure the guy with the baseball cap was no longer following her, Jessica rode the elevator back up to the fifth floor. Her ego had really received a blow. She and Mr. Gorgeous had stood only inches apart; he had had a perfect opportunity to notice how attractive she was. *She* had noticed that he was even better-looking than she'd thought, and older, too, probably a recent college graduate. But he had sprinted away from her without a second glance! *I might as well have been a hideous old bag lady for all he cared,* Jessica thought dejectedly.

Seated at her desk a few minutes later, she shuffled through the papers in her in box. "Proofreading, proofreading, and more proofreading," she muttered.

"Hey, Jessica," someone said from the doorway.

She spun around on her chair. "Oh, hi, Bill."

He flashed her one of his movie-star smiles. "I just wanted to check in with you. Got enough to keep you busy?"

"More than enough," she answered.

"Good. Stay out of trouble, Jess."

She laughed wryly. "Somehow I doubt I'll get in any trouble proofreading an article about a regatta at the Sweet Valley Yacht Club."

Bill chuckled. "Sounds like heavy stuff. See you at the story meeting later."

"You sure will."

As soon as Bill was gone Jessica picked up the telephone. Maggie was talking to her friend Val. She told Val that she was afraid her husband was starting to suspect something. "It was bound to happen sooner or later," Jessica lectured Maggie. "With all the running around you do!"

Sighing, Jessica replaced the receiver. She just wasn't in the mood for Maggie's dilemma today.

Propping her elbows on the desk, Jessica rested her chin in her hands and stared glumly out the window. The cute blond guy was also sitting at his desk, completely absorbed in his work—and completely oblivious of the fact that Jessica was watching him from across the street. *What a rotten day this has been so far*, Jessica thought. *I get followed by creepy guys, and cute guys run away from me!*

Just then, the blond guy looked up—and straight at Jessica. For a long moment, they stared at each other. Then, slowly, a smile spread across his face.

He recognizes me from the lobby! Jessica realized, a huge smile lighting up her own face. *Now he knows why I gave him that line about knowing him from somewhere!*

All at once, he appeared a lot friendlier than he had after their collision outside the coffee shop. In fact, Jessica decided, his smile was downright inviting. It was now or never. Grabbing a blank sheet of paper, she scrawled her name and the phone number of the *News* in giant block letters. Then she held the paper up to the window.

She held her breath. Could he read what she had written from all the way across the street? Would he make the next move and call her or would he blow her off again?

She saw him reach for something. The phone! A few seconds later, her own phone rang. Jessica picked it up eagerly. "Is this Jessica?" an unbelievably deep and sexy voice asked.

"Yes. And you must be . . ."

"Ben Donovan. The guy on the fifth floor of the Bank Building who's so wrapped up in his work that he almost missed the chance to meet a pretty girl on the fifth floor of the Western Building."

They smiled at each other through their respective windows.

"Sorry about almost trampling you down in the lobby earlier," he went on. "I had an appointment. I'm not usually that abrupt."

"Well, I'd be happy to let you make it up to me," Jessica said suggestively.

"Let me take you out for coffee after work today," Ben urged.

Jessica was suffused with happiness. "I'll meet you on the sidewalk at five o'clock," she told him. And silently she added, *I thought you'd never ask!*

"I've been worrying about you all day," Elizabeth said, dropping her purse and notepad on her desk a few minutes before five.

"Worrying about me? Why?"

Jessica was gazing at herself in a compact mirror and touching up her lip gloss and mascara. Elizabeth stared at her. "Well, you were so spooked all weekend," she explained. "Because of the murder, and those hang-up phone calls."

"Well, I'm not spooked anymore," Jessica declared. She beamed at her twin. "Guess who I finally made contact with?"

"It can't be Greenback," Elizabeth kidded. "So it must be Mr. Gorgeous."

"What a good investigative reporter you'll make someday!" Jessica ran a brush through her glossy blond hair. "We have a date in three minutes. Oh, look!" Jessica pointed out the window. "He's not in his office! He's already on his way down to the street to meet me!"

Elizabeth sank into her desk chair. "Well, have a good time."

It suddenly occurred to Jessica to ask Elizabeth how *her* day had gone. "You look beat, Liz. Any breakthroughs on the story?"

"None." Elizabeth sighed. "The police still haven't identified the body. There's just not a lot to go on."

"Well, I'd love to stay and chat, but—"

The phone on Jessica's desk rang. She picked it up. "Jessica Wakefield speaking."

"Jessica, it's Detective Jason at the station."

"Hi, Detective Jason," Jessica said, her voice low. She gestured to Elizabeth to close the door to their office so no one in the newsroom could hear her.

"I just wanted to check in with you. Did you hear any more delivery-service messages today?"

"Not one," Jessica informed him. "The murderers must be keeping a low profile since the discovery of the body," she added knowingly. Then she remembered the disconcerting incident that had slipped her mind in her euphoria over Ben Donovan. "I think someone may have been following me during my lunch hour, though." Jessica described the man in the baseball cap.

"Don't worry, we'll keep an eye out for him," Detective Jason assured her. "I'll touch base with you again tomorrow, Jessica. Don't forget to be very careful—and very discreet. You should be keeping a low profile yourself."

"I am," she promised. "Thanks, Detective Jason." She replaced the receiver.

"What did he say?" Elizabeth asked. "And why didn't you tell me that someone followed you?"

"It wasn't a big deal," Jessica said, brushing off the lunch-hour incident. "Detective Jason just told me to keep doing what I've been doing— you know, eavesdropping. And he told me I should keep a low profile."

"He's right," Elizabeth asserted. "Don't go blabbing about this to anybody, Jess. Not even your new boyfriend from across the street."

"I told you not to worry," Jessica reminded her twin. "Do you want to walk out with me?"

Elizabeth shook her head. "I promised Seth I'd make a few more phone calls for him. We got so caught up in this murder story that we're behind on the rest of our research. Have fun."

"Don't work too hard!" Jessica counseled as she breezed out of the office.

She could hardly wait to get outside. Crossing the lobby, she caught a glimpse of her reflection in the coffee shop's plate glass window. What a lucky break that she had worn her new jade-green knit minidress and black blazer to work that day. *I really look sharp*, Jessica thought with satisfaction.

Ben Donovan had crossed the street and was waiting for her by the entrance to the Western Building. As she pushed through the revolving door Jessica admired his appearance. He looked casually elegant with his suit jacket slung over his shoulder and his tie slightly loosened; a light tan set off his bright blond hair and blue eyes. *We make such a glamorous couple!* Jessica thought. She was sure that everyone on the sidewalk must be staring at them with admiration and envy.

"Jessica, it's nice to meet you—officially." Ben took her hand and gave it a businesslike shake.

Jessica squeezed his hand in return. "It's nice to finally meet *you*," she said, fluttering her eyelashes.

"What do you say we walk over to Pacific Avenue?" he suggested. "I love the appetizers at the Leeward Isles."

The Leeward Isles was a popular new restaurant. Jessica loved their appetizers, too, and she loved the fact that Ben was obviously hoping their cup of coffee after work would develop into a romantic candlelit dinner for two.

As they strolled to the restaurant Jessica studied her date. In the bright late afternoon sunlight, she could see that he was definitely a little older than she had thought at first—maybe as old as twenty-five. But he would never guess she was only sixteen. Jessica knew she could be mistaken for someone older, especially when she was dressed up.

Soon they were seated at a secluded table at the Leeward Isles. "So, Jessica," Ben began.

She smiled at him encouragingly, waiting for the inevitable question: *Where have you been all my life?*

"How long have you been working at the *News?*"

Jessica blinked. What kind of question was that? Well, she supposed an icebreaker was an icebreaker. They had to start someplace. "I'm a summer intern," she replied, careful not to mention that she was only a high-school student. He would probably assume she was in college.

"What kind of things do you do there?"

"Oh, I'm just a gofer," Jessica said briskly. She really wanted to move on from this boring topic to more interesting personal areas. "I help reporters with their research and I do some copyediting and proofreading. Whatever Bill Anderson—he's the news editor—tells me to do."

"It must be exciting, working at a newspaper," Ben commented.

"It's not bad," Jessica admitted. "This murder case has us all in an uproar."

"Hmm. I'm sure it does."

"What about you?" Jessica leaned forward. "What do you do over there in the Bank Building? You always look so busy and important!"

Ben chuckled. "Busy, yes. I'm an accountant."

"An accountant?" Jessica wondered if her disappointment was obvious. She had been hoping for a lawyer, or at least a banker. An accountant was about the dullest thing she could imagine!

"That's right," said Ben. "I'm new to Young

and Biddle, but I'm pleased with the position so far. It's a solid, respectable firm."

Solid and *respectable* were Jessica's two least favorite adjectives. "Oh," she replied.

Then she caught herself. Of course, Ben had to do *something* for a living. *I bet he really cuts loose in his spare time*, Jessica speculated hopefully. Conservative businessman by day, romantic adventurer by night!

"What are your hobbies?" she asked hopefully. "What do you do on the weekends?" He just had to be an avid windsurfer or mountain climber; maybe he even played guitar in a rock band.

"I'm kind of a quiet guy," Ben confessed. "I like to go jogging with my Dalmatian, catch up on my reading, listen to classical music, watch old movies."

"Oh," Jessica said again. Just thinking about it made her want to yawn!

They ordered a couple of appetizers, and Jessica began thinking up excuses for why she couldn't stay for dinner as well. Who would have thought Mr. Gorgeous would have turned out to be so nice and down-to-earth and *boring?*

He's Liz's type, not mine, Jessica concluded ruefully as they left the restaurant half an hour later. Besides, he was too old for either of them! All he had wanted to know about Jessica was what she thought of her job at the newspaper. She might as well have been out for a date with Detective Jason!

Ben walked Jessica back to the parking lot next to the Western Building. "That was fun," Jessica lied as they shook hands again.

"I'll call you sometime," Ben said.

"I'd like that," Jessica fibbed.

As she told him her phone number, though, she had a distinct feeling that he had just asked for it out of politeness. She probably wouldn't hear from him. *And that's OK with me,* Jessica thought as she waved goodbye to Mr. Gorgeous. Reality was so much less exciting than fantasy!

Seven

When Elizabeth and Jessica arrived at the newsroom on Tuesday, they found a crowd of reporters, editors, and assistants gathered around the police-band radio. Ordinarily, the reports were pretty mundane—news of traffic accidents, an occasional burglary. But this morning, a hum of excited voices almost drowned out the sound of the broadcast.

"What's happening?" Jessica demanded.

Seth turned to them, his eyes bright. Elizabeth knew that look; a story was breaking, and it was a good one.

"They've identified the body found on the beach," he informed the twins. "Just as I predicted, she was a runaway. Seventeen-year-old Tracy Fox from San Diego."

"Only seventeen years old!" Elizabeth exclaimed. "How sad."

"Not much older than we are," Jessica said soberly.

"You're still my partner on this story," Seth told Elizabeth. "Someone needs to head over to the station to get more details. But someone else should jump right on the telephone and try to make contact with Tracy Fox's parents. I know it's been less than twenty-four hours since the police broke the news to them, but we've got to get some background, see if we can discover anything that might help us figure out how she ended up the way she did."

Seth studied Elizabeth's face. She knew her feelings showed.

"It's going to be a tough phone call," he continued. "How about I send you to the station with Anita, Liz? I'll stay here and make the call."

"No, you go to the station," Elizabeth urged him. "Let me make the call, Seth."

"You're a good interviewer," Seth said. "But are you sure you can handle this assignment?"

"Yes," Elizabeth said firmly. "I want to make part of this story my own. You can trust me to do a good job, Seth."

"I know I can count on you, Liz. OK, go for it! And don't worry. If Tracy Fox's parents don't want to talk to the press, they'll tell you so."

With Jessica at her side, Elizabeth walked to her desk. She looked at her telephone uncertainly. She was eager to help Seth and thrilled to be allowed so much responsibility. But suddenly, Elizabeth was a little sorry she had talked Seth into letting her conduct this interview.

"I'm not sure I want to do this after all," she said to her twin. "I mean, think about it, Jess. What if one of us had been murdered? Imagine how Mom and Dad would feel having reporters hounding them."

"It's called investigative journalism," Jessica reminded her. "You love it—that's why you're doing this summer internship!"

"I know. I just never expected to be working on a story like this." Elizabeth shook her head. "OK. I might as well get to it."

Elizabeth dialed the number of Tracy Fox's parents in San Diego. Jessica perched on the edge of her sister's desk, listening eagerly. The phone rang two times, three, four. *Good*, Elizabeth thought, relieved. *They're not home, or they're not answering. I'll just—*

Just as she was about to hang up, someone picked up the phone. "Hello?"

The man's tone was wary. Elizabeth guessed that the Foxes' phone had probably been ringing off the hook. "Is this Mr. Fox?" she said.

"It is."

"Mr. Fox, my name is Elizabeth Wakefield. I'm on the staff of the *Sweet Valley News*. I'd like to express the sympathy of everyone here on the death of your daughter, Tracy."

"Thank you." Mr. Fox's voice was gruff. "But I suppose that's not the only reason you called."

"No," she admitted. "I'd like to ask you a few questions about Tracy. But if you'd rather not talk—"

"Let me get my wife," Mr. Fox offered. "She's better at this sort of thing than I am."

When Mrs. Fox came on the phone, Elizabeth introduced herself again, and again expressed her sympathy. "Mrs. Fox, I know it must be difficult for you to talk about your daughter so soon after . . . But I'd appreciate it if you took a moment to speak with me."

Mrs. Fox cleared her throat. It sounded as if she was very close to tears and struggling to maintain self-control. "Tracy's father and I are devastated. We have two younger children, but Tracy was our only daughter—our oldest child. But to tell you the truth, Ms. Wakefield, in some ways we felt as if we'd lost her months ago."

"What do you mean?" Elizabeth prodded gently.

"Ever since she ran away from home a month ago, we've been afraid—we've been waiting for the bad news," Mrs. Fox explained. "You see, Tracy was always a straight-A student, a sweet, quiet girl. But a year ago, she fell in with a bad crowd at school. I'm still not sure I understand how it happened—or why it happened. But it was like a wall had been put up between us. We couldn't reach her. She would go to these wild parties and stay out all night. The kids at the parties did drugs. Her father and I both knew that. We tried disciplining her and talking to her about what was going on, warning her that she could hurt herself. But the more we tried to guide her, the more she pulled away from us."

"It must have been a very difficult time for you," Elizabeth said sympathetically.

"It was. And the worst of all was the last night she was home. I was folding laundry, and I went to put some of Tracy's clothes away in her dresser. I found . . . I found a packet of cocaine in one of her drawers. I confronted her with it. It was the first real evidence we'd had that she was using drugs. I was so shocked, and so scared."

Elizabeth gasped. "How awful."

"We had a terrible fight. And the next morning, Tracy was gone. We never saw her or heard from her again." Mrs. Fox's voice broke off. To Elizabeth's dismay, she could hear the other woman crying quietly. "My heart breaks when I think that we never really got to say goodbye to her, that our last words were spoken in anger."

Elizabeth's own eyes brimmed with tears. "I'm so sorry, Mrs. Fox," she murmured.

"I can't tell you anything more, Ms. Wakefield. We just don't know anything more."

"You've been very helpful," Elizabeth assured her. "Thank you for speaking with me, Mrs. Fox."

Slowly, Elizabeth replaced the receiver. Jessica peered at her face. "Liz, you're crying!"

"It's such a sad story." Elizabeth took the tissue Jessica handed her and blew her nose. "Poor Mr. and Mrs. Fox. Poor Tracy."

"Well, tell me!" Jessica bounced on the desk. "What happened? Why did Tracy run away?"

Before Elizabeth could reply, Seth, already back from the police station, burst into their office. "Wait till you hear this, guys!" he exclaimed. "There was something about Tracy that the police didn't release at first. A packet of cocaine was found in the pocket of the jacket she was wearing when her body was found. They're sure the killing was drug-related."

Jessica gasped. "Drug-related!"

"That fits in with what Mrs. Fox just told me," Elizabeth confirmed.

"It does?" Jessica whirled on her twin. "Why didn't you tell me?"

"I was just about to!" Quickly, Elizabeth recounted her conversation with Mr. and Mrs. Fox.

Seth whistled. "Poor kid. She really took the wrong road. She must have been dealing. She had to support herself somehow after she ran away, and I guess drugs seemed like an easy way out."

"An easy way out that cost her her life," Elizabeth reflected solemnly.

"Dealing drugs . . ." Jessica mused. Suddenly, she stared at her twin. "That explains it!" she burst out. "The delivery-service calls," she whispered in Elizabeth's ear. "The *packets*!"

"Explains what?" Seth asked, looking from one girl to the other. "What are you whispering about?"

Elizabeth glanced at Seth. The police obviously had not said anything to the press about Jessica's involvement or about the phone calls she had overheard. It made sense. Detective Jason had promised Jessica that in the interest of protecting her, they would not release her name. And it wouldn't do for Greenback's messages to become public. If he knew his cover had been blown, he would be on the defensive, and the police would have a much harder time tracking him down.

Elizabeth would have liked to confide in Seth, but she knew it was better and safer to cooperate with the police's request for secrecy. "Nothing," Elizabeth said firmly. "Just something Jessica and I were talking about before. So, Seth," she added quickly, "where do we go from here?"

"First, we write up what we've got for tomorrow's paper," Seth replied. "Then we try to find out more about Tracy Fox. You've learned about her life in San Diego, her life with her family. What's still a big blank, though, is exactly where she lived and what she did in the month between the day she ran away from home and the day she died."

"And who she knew," Elizabeth added.

"Right. Think about it while I draft this article,

Liz," Seth requested. "We can talk about our strategy over lunch."

As soon as they had the office to themselves, Jessica gripped her twin's arm. "Liz! Do you know what this means?"

Elizabeth nodded. "The delivery service really *is* some kind of drug ring."

"Tracy knew Greenback and Rock," Jessica declared. "And for some reason they killed her."

"It's horrible!" Elizabeth cried. "That poor, stupid girl. Oh, Jess, I hate thinking about it. It reminds me of what happened to Regina Morrow. Drugs are so destructive. Why would anyone get involved with them?"

Regina Morrow had been a classmate and friend of the twins at Sweet Valley High. Upset because her boyfriend had just broken up with her, Regina had started hanging out with some kids who did drugs. One night at a party, she was pressured into trying cocaine and had died of cardiac arrest after experiencing a rare reaction to the drug. Regina's sudden death had been a harsh and tragic lesson to the other students at Sweet Valley High, and it was a lesson that the Wakefield twins would never forget.

"It's *hard* being a teenager sometimes," Jessica said, her expression uncharacteristically serious. "You can get on the wrong path, choose the wrong role models. And it happens so quickly!"

"I wish someone had been able to help

Regina," Elizabeth reflected. "I wish someone had helped Tracy."

"It's too late for them now," Jessica said sadly.

Suddenly, Elizabeth felt a new, urgent sense of commitment to the Tracy Fox case. "It *is* too late for them," she agreed. "But there are a lot of other young people out there at risk. I'm going to dig into this case," she vowed. "I'm going to help crack this story so maybe I can help some of *them*."

At home after dinner that night, Elizabeth went upstairs to her room, propped the pillows up on her bed, and settled back to work. She opened the manila folder she had brought home with her from work. Inside was all the information she and Seth had gathered so far about Tracy Fox.

She thumbed through the papers. "What's this?" she said out loud.

In the back of the folder was a color photograph of Tracy Fox. She hadn't noticed it when Seth gave her the material at the office. Noting the lace-collared blouse and delicate gold necklace Tracy wore, Elizabeth deduced it was a formal yearbook picture.

Elizabeth studied the sweet freckled face in the photo, the wide-set green eyes and fluffy fair hair. *Just another all-American girl*, she thought. *She could be me or Jess, or any one of our friends.*

Then a strange sensation flooded Elizabeth,

making her skin crawl. Tracy was a stranger, a girl from another town, another school, a girl Elizabeth could never have laid eyes on. And yet with an intense shock, Elizabeth realized that she had seen her face somewhere before.

"Jessica!" Elizabeth hollered at the top of her lungs.

Jessica came galloping through the bathroom that connected the twins' bedrooms. "What's the matter?" she cried.

"This picture." Elizabeth handed it to Jessica. "Look at this picture!"

Jessica took the photograph. She wrinkled her forehead. "Is this Tracy Fox?"

"Yes." Elizabeth took a deep breath, trying to slow her pounding heart. "What do you think about it?"

"She's pretty," said Jessica. "Wow, it's so sad. I mean, it was sad before, having someone die. But now that we know who she is and what she looks like—"

"But do you recognize her?" Elizabeth pressed. "Does she look familiar to you?"

Jessica shook her head. "No. No, she doesn't."

"Well, she looks familiar to *me*," Elizabeth told her twin. "Jessica, I've seen Tracy Fox somewhere before!"

Jessica bounced onto the bed next to her sister. "You have?" she squealed. "Where? When?"

"That's what I'm not sure about." Elizabeth frowned. "I've seen her though—I'm positive of that. And it was recently, not long before her death. But I just can't remember. . . ."

"Think, Liz!" Jessica urged. "Think hard!"

Elizabeth concentrated with all her might. Then she shook her head with a sigh. "Maybe it'll come to me."

Just then the phone rang. Elizabeth picked up the extension on her night table, her heart leaping with expectation. Maybe it was Todd, calling from his family camping trip in the Canadian Rockies.

"Hello?" she said eagerly. She heard breathing, but no one spoke. "Hello?" she repeated. "Who is this?"

A moment later, the line was disconnected. Elizabeth shrugged. "Oh well," she said nonchalantly. "A wrong number, I suppose."

But Jessica, who had been watching her twin very carefully, suddenly turned pale. "It's them," she whispered, clutching Elizabeth's arm.

"Who?"

"The people who killed Tracy," Jessica answered ominously.

Elizabeth stared at her sister. *The people who killed Tracy.* The words hung in the air like cold, dark shadows.

Elizabeth shuddered. "Of course it wasn't the people who killed Tracy," she said matter-of-factly. "Jess, you know it couldn't be. The police still haven't determined that the phone calls you overheard are connected with Tracy's death.

Even if they are, the murderers have no way—*no way*," she repeated, "of knowing anyone's been listening in on their conversations. And certainly no way of knowing that that someone is Jessica Wakefield of Calico Drive in Sweet Valley!"

"You really think so?" Jessica asked hopefully.

"I really think so," Elizabeth confirmed. "Only our family and the police know about what you're doing. You're perfectly safe, safer than ever with the Sweet Valley police force on your side."

Jessica nodded. "I guess so," she said in a small voice. But something about the apprehensive way she glanced at the telephone, now sitting quietly on the night table, told Elizabeth that Jessica was not convinced.

And even though her argument was completely rational, Elizabeth herself did not feel entirely at ease. Suddenly she felt vulnerable and scared, sitting alone with her twin in the quiet house. Something terrible had happened in their usually idyllic community. And somehow, Elizabeth and Jessica were right in the middle of it.

Eight

Bill Anderson was waiting for Jessica and Elizabeth when they arrived at work on Wednesday morning. "Have I got a job for you," he said to Jessica as she stepped into the newsroom.

"Let me guess. You're making me editor-in-chief?" Jessica quipped. "It's about time!"

Bill grinned. "No, something you'll like even better." Taking her arm, he steered her through the already bustling newsroom to her and Elizabeth's office.

"Rose quit," he told the twins.

"She quit?" Elizabeth said in surprise. "Rose has been the receptionist here for years!"

"Yep," Bill confirmed. "But a better job came

her way. So this morning, I was thinking about how to handle the situation while we search for a new permanent replacement. I thought, who in this office loves to spend time on the telephone?"

Suddenly, Jessica saw what was coming.

Bill gestured toward her desk. "Ta-da!"

The receptionist's telephone console had been installed on Jessica's desk. She wrinkled her nose at it. "Look at all those buttons," she groaned.

"This is only temporary," Bill reiterated. "I know you signed on here this summer to learn how to be a reporter and writer, not how to talk on the phone."

"Yeah, she already knew how to do *that*," Elizabeth agreed with a mischievous smile.

Jessica shot her twin a deadly glance.

"It won't be too bad. You'll still have the privacy of your office, so in between taking and forwarding calls you can work on copyediting and proofreading." Bill handed Jessica a sheet of paper. "Here's a list of everyone's title and extension number. Just route the calls to the appropriate party, and if you get one you can't handle, pass it on to me or Lawrence Robb, the features editor. Oh, and I guess you won't be needing this." Bill walked over to Jessica's desk and unplugged her old telephone. He tucked it under his arm. "Well, go to it, Jess. Put that gift of gab to good use!"

Jessica managed a weak smile. "Looks like I don't have much choice."

"Help me out with this and I'll make it up to you," Bill said as he turned to leave.

Jessica liked the sound of that. Her smile grew warmer. "OK, boss."

Just then, the phone began buzzing insistently. Three calls were coming in at once. Jessica picked up the first line. "Good morning, the *News*, can you hold?" She hit the hold button, then took the second call. "Good morning, the *News*, can you hold?" Repeating the procedure, she picked up the third line. "Good morning, the *News*, how can I help you?" she said breathlessly.

After Jessica transferred all three calls, Elizabeth shook her head. "No offense, Jess, but I'm sure glad I'm not you this morning."

"Thanks a lot, Liz," Jessica said sarcastically. "It's always nice to get such great moral support from my devoted sister."

Elizabeth grinned. "And I'm also glad I'm going to be out with Anita, researching a story," she added. "This 'Good morning, the *News*, can you hold?' routine could really drive a person crazy!"

Elizabeth wasn't kidding about going crazy, Jessica thought later that morning. Now she knew why Rose had quit! The phone rang constantly. Half the calls were wrong numbers, intended for someplace else in the building, a result of the general phone service mess. *If I get one more call for Wells and Wells, the law firm on the seventh floor, or Steadman's Insurance on the third, I think I'll scream!* Jessica thought, gritting her teeth.

She took an incoming call. "No, this is *not* Fawn at the coffee shop," she snapped, feeling that scream rising in her throat. "And no, I do *not* know what today's lunch specials are!"

She slammed down the receiver. Immediately, the phone rang again. This time it was a call for Seth. Jessica tried to put it through, but his extension was busy. What was Seth doing on the phone? Jessica had expected him to be out of the office, chasing down information about Tracy Fox. "I'll have to take a message," she told the caller grumpily.

She scribbled down the information and added it to the small pile of messages she had taken so far that morning. At least half of them were for Seth. It seemed as if he had been on his phone all morning! A giggle burst from Jessica as a funny thought struck her. Maybe Seth was really Junior, the guy who got lectured by his mother twenty times a day!

The phone rang again. As she picked it up Jessica swiveled in her chair just in time to see Bill peeking in at her. She sat up a little straighter and tossed back her hair. "Good morning, *Sweet Valley News*," she said in her most efficient, professional manner. "Can I help you?"

Bill gave her a thumbs-up sign. Jessica could tell he was pleased to see her looking so busy.

When Bill moved off into the newsroom, Jessica turned back toward the window. The current caller was requesting information about newspaper subscriptions, so she transferred him to Gwen, the subscription manager. Then she took three more calls in quick succession. In the middle of that flurry, Jessica glanced up to see Ben Donovan watching her from his office across the street. He smiled and she gave him a distracted wave.

Finally, Jessica could see by the clock over the door that it was almost noon. Beth, one of the other interns, was going to cover for her while she took a lunch break. *And do I ever need a break!* Jessica thought.

She waited for the phone to ring. She didn't even dare stretch; she knew the minute she relaxed, she would be inundated with calls. But miraculously, the phone remained quiet. For the first time that morning, Jessica had the leisure to remember something: her own phone line and the delivery-service calls! As far as Jessica could tell, Greenback had been silent since the discovery of Tracy's body. But what if he had resumed his criminal conversations?

Bill had unplugged her phone. *Hmm*, Jessica mused. What would happen if she dialed her own extension from the receptionist's phone? She knew it was a long shot, but there was no reason not to try. Picking up the receiver, she punched in her extension number. All she heard was a dial tone. But on the second try, she heard a voice: Junior's. It had worked! She could access her line from the switchboard and listen in to other people's conversations!

A few seconds later, Jessica had to hang up on Junior in order to take an incoming call. But as soon as the line was clear again she tapped back into her extension. This time, she heard Greenback's voice.

He seemed to be giving an ordinary delivery message, meaningless to Jessica. Nevertheless, she knew it could be important to Detective Jason. If Greenback's organization was really a drug ring, as Jessica was convinced, all the police had to do was crack the code and then they could catch Greenback's gang in the act!

I should write the message down, Jessica thought. She searched her cluttered desk for the message pad. Then her eyes came to rest on the dictaphone, and she had an even better idea.

Rapidly, she slipped in a new cassette. Then, holding the dictaphone's tiny microphone close to the receiver, she hit the record button. Would it work?

Greenback concluded his conversation with the man named Chopper. Jessica hit the stop button on the dictaphone and rewound the tape. She glanced around to make sure there was nobody watching her. Then she put on the headphones and hit play. Sure enough, she had recorded Greenback's voice! "Delivery at point two, eight o'clock," he had said. "Delivery at point six, ten o'clock. Red fish, white water."

Point two, point six, red fish, white water. It didn't make any sense to Jessica. But it very well might be useful to the police. *For the rest of the day, whenever I can, I'll keep eavesdropping and taping the messages,* Jessica decided. Then after work, she would drop the tape off with Detective Jason at the station. With her help, the police were sure to solve the case in no time!

After spending the morning helping Anita, Elizabeth burst into Seth's office a few minutes after twelve. Seth was talking on the phone, but when he saw Elizabeth, he quickly cut the conversation short. At the same time, he took a file of some sort and shoved it in his desk drawer.

"What have you got?" he asked her briskly.

"I've got some sandwiches," Elizabeth replied, displaying the bag from the deli, "*and* I've got an idea." She pulled up a chair next to his. "An idea about how we might learn something about Tracy's acquaintances and activities during the month she was a runaway." She handed Seth a ham and cheese sandwich.

"OK, let's hear it," he said before taking a big bite.

Elizabeth had been thinking that if Tracy's photograph had given her a jolt, maybe it would jog somebody else's memory, too. She told Seth her idea. "We print Tracy's picture in the *News*, with a request that anyone who had contact with her or who has any information about her acquaintances should call us. There just *have* to be people out there who knew her, who could help us!"

Seth crunched into a pickle. "I wouldn't count on it, Liz. Most likely, Tracy was a loner. We know she knew some drug dealers—and at least one murderer. Those folks aren't about to turn themselves in! And if she did have any friends, well, they'd be druggy, down-and-out types, too. They'd be afraid to come forward because they'd be afraid of getting busted."

Seth's words were discouraging. But Elizabeth was not ready to give up. "It's worth a try," she insisted.

Seth studied her earnest face. Finally, he nodded. "You're right, Liz. It's worth a try. Anything's worth a try. Write up the copy. We'll put the plea on the front page of tomorrow's paper."

By the end of the day, Jessica's nerves were stretched to the breaking point. She hoped Bill would hire a new permanent receptionist, to work the switchboard, and fast!

There were so many incoming calls, she had not been able to eavesdrop on her own line very often. Even so, she had managed to pick up on two delivery-service messages. Now, with the lines momentarily quiet, Jessica accessed her own extension one more time.

What luck—it was the delivery service! Quickly, Jessica pressed the record button on the dictaphone and positioned the microphone close to her ear.

The conversation was difficult to hear. It was being conducted in hoarse whispers, and there was background noise—a computer printer or some other kind of machine was clattering loudly. Even so, Jessica was able to identify the voices of Greenback and Rock.

"They're on to us," Rock told Greenback as Jessica listened. His voice was rough and angry. "Our buddy at the police station says they've assigned a special undercover cop. The whole thing is very hush-hush—no one at the station knows who or where he is. But the word is, he's closing in on us."

The news of an undercover cop was a great surprise to Jessica. But it was something else Rock had said that caused her body to go stiff with shock. Rock had referred to "our buddy at the police station." Did that mean someone on the police force was helping the drug dealers instead of hunting them?

Jessica strained her ears to hear Greenback's response. "We'll need to be extra careful," Greenback warned his colleague. "Get out of Sweet Valley, and we'll meet at point six in a week to divide the cash. Then we'll close up shop and break up the organization."

"First, let me take care of the nosy girl," Rock

said. The evil eagerness in his voice sent a chill running up Jessica's spine.

"No, I've got my eye on her," Greenback told Rock. "She's not spying today, I guarantee it. Just leave her to me. I'll handle her when the time comes."

Click. The call ended.

With a robotlike motion, Jessica replaced the receiver and turned off the dictaphone. She couldn't believe what she had just heard. Greenback had ordered Rock to leave Sweet Valley—beyond a shadow of a doubt, then, the drug ring was operating right there in town!

Right here in Sweet Valley, Jessica thought. *It could even involve people I know!* She cast a terrified glance over her shoulder. *People who work in the Western Building!*

Jessica sat limply in her chair, devastated by her discovery. A drug ring in Sweet Valley—and someone at the police station was leaking information to its leaders. It was too horrible to contemplate.

But worst of all had been the final exchange between the two men. Slipping on the headphone, Jessica replayed the conversation on the dictaphone. The ominous words pierced her heart like needles of ice. The nosy girl, the one Rock wanted to "take care of" . . . Jessica's teeth suddenly started to chatter. The girl Greenback had his eye on, that he was going to "handle" when the time came—*could it be me?* At this horrible thought, Jessica felt herself struck by a wave of dread as strong as the one that had washed over her that day on the beach at Castle Cove, when she had glimpsed Tracy's dead body.

The phone buzzed, and Jessica jumped. She picked up the receiver gingerly. "G-good afternoon, the *N-news*," she stuttered.

"I'd like to speak with Jessica Wakefield. This is Detective Jason of the Sweet Valley police."

"Oh, it's me, Detective Jason," Jessica breathed, immensely relieved to hear his deep, authoritative voice.

"Just checking in," he said. "Do you have any more information for me?"

Jessica was about to blurt out that she had been taping Greenback's conversations on her dictaphone. Then she stopped herself as a terrible doubt entered her mind.

Can I trust him? she wondered, biting her lip. There was a bad cop at the police station; one of Greenback and Rock's friends was on the Sweet Valley force. What if it was Detective Jason?

"I—I haven't heard anything all day," Jessica lied. "I'm the receptionist for the whole newspaper now, so I'm using a different telephone. I—I can't eavesdrop on Greenback's calls anymore."

To her surprise and relief, Detective Jason didn't question this. "I understand," he said. "Let's keep in touch, though."

"Sure," Jessica agreed. Shaking, she replaced

the receiver. She wondered if she had done the right thing. Detective Jason was trying to solve the case, wasn't he? He needed her help, didn't he? He probably wasn't the bad cop. But even so, Jessica knew she could not risk telling him, or anyone at the police station, about the conversation she had just overheard. By revealing what she knew, she would be putting herself in serious jeopardy. Jessica had no idea how Greenback and Rock could have found out about her, if indeed they had. *But if they know who I am, and if they find out I'm still listening, they'll kill me, just like they killed Tracy.*

Jessica had never been so frightened in her entire life. She had thought Detective Jason was her ally. Over the course of the past few days, she had felt more secure knowing she was in contact with the police. But now she couldn't trust them for protection. And what if Rock didn't listen to Greenback? What if he came after her anyway?

Jessica jumped to her feet. She couldn't stand being in the office a minute longer, with Elizabeth off working on the Tracy Fox story with Seth. Jessica checked the clock over the door. It was almost five. She was entitled to leave. Grabbing her things, she sprinted across the newsroom to the hall and the elevator.

As she rode down to the main floor, Jessica decided she would shop in town for a while and then take the bus home. She would leave the Jeep for Elizabeth; she wouldn't be able to get up her courage enough to enter the gloomy parking garage by herself. In the lobby, Jessica walked quickly, looking straight ahead. She just wanted to get out on the sidewalk, into the sunshine.

Suddenly, Jessica felt a heavy hand on her shoulder. She jumped, biting back a scream.

Ben Donovan stared down at her. "Jessica, are you all right?" he asked, his blue eyes warm with concern. "I couldn't help noticing that you looked incredibly busy and hassled today. Can I buy you a cup of coffee?"

Jessica didn't know whether to be relieved or anxious at the sight of Ben. Part of her was tempted to take him up on his offer. No one would bother her while she was with him. Maybe she could even tell him what was going on. It would help to get an outsider's advice.

But simultaneously, Jessica found herself feeling suspicious of Ben. He was popping up all over the place lately. And why was he watching her so carefully from across the street? Were his intentions toward her really friendly and innocent?

Even if she wanted to confide in Ben, Jessica knew she couldn't risk it. Detective Jason had warned her not to share her knowledge with anyone. And Jessica could not forget Greenback's last remark: "I've got my eye on her."

Jessica glanced fearfully around the crowded lobby. For all she knew, Greenback or one of his associates was watching her right now. One false step and she could wash up on the beach like Tracy Fox.

"Thanks, Ben, but I can't. I've got to—" Jessica didn't finish her sentence. With another panicked look around her, she dashed out of the building.

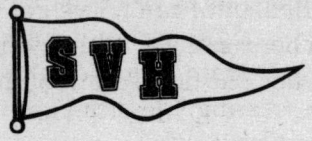

Nine

"You wouldn't believe the day I had!" Jessica announced to her sister when Elizabeth finally got home at about nine o'clock on Wednesday night.

"Mine was pretty hectic, too." With a tired sigh, Elizabeth sank into a chair at the table in the Wakefields' Spanish-tiled kitchen. "Seth and I drove all the way to San Diego and back this afternoon. We were looking for a personal angle on the Tracy Fox story, so we decided to interview some of Tracy's old high school friends, the kids she was hanging out with before she ran away."

Reaching up, Elizabeth removed the ponytail holder from her hair and shook it loose. "Jessica, it was so depressing. I just didn't understand their attitude. I mean, they said they were bummed out when Tracy ran away, and I could see they were really sad about her being killed. But they didn't seem to see her death as any kind of warning about what could happen to them if they don't go straight and quit the drug scene." Elizabeth sighed again. "I just don't get it."

"That *is* depressing," Jessica agreed. "But, Liz, let me tell you about—"

She was interrupted by the phone ringing. Jessica hesitated momentarily before answering it. "Hello?" As Elizabeth watched, her twin's wary expression gave way to a relaxed smile. "Oh, hi, Todd! Yep, she's right here."

Todd! Elizabeth leaped to her feet, her energy suddenly returning. Jessica tossed her the receiver. "Hi!" Elizabeth cried. "How are you?"

"Hi, Liz," Todd said. "Boy, it's good to hear your voice!"

Tears sprang to Elizabeth's eyes. "It's good to hear yours, too," she said softly. She wished so much that he weren't so far away. She would have loved to talk to him in person about the Tracy Fox case and to feel his strong, comforting arms around her. "Where are you?" she asked, determined not to get too emotional, especially since Jessica had made no move to leave the room.

"At a pay phone near our campsite. I used my calling card," Todd replied. "It's not exactly the ideal place for a private conversation. Probably just as well, though. This way I won't be tempted to get too mushy and go on and on about how much I miss you. I do, though. A whole lot."

"I miss you, too," Elizabeth told him.

"I just really wish you could see this place, Liz! Today we hiked along this little lake high up in the mountains. It was like a jewel, as clear and green as an emerald. Everything is just so clean and beautiful. And there's all sorts of wildlife—mountain goats, bald eagles, bears. Yesterday, I canoed right up to some moose wading in a stream to drink. Luckily I had my camera, so you'll get to see the photographic evidence!"

"It sounds like you're having fun," she said wistfully. "I sure wish *I* could get away from it all! You wouldn't believe what's been going on in Sweet Valley, Todd." She gave him a complete update on the Tracy Fox murder.

"That's really awful," Todd exclaimed. "Liz, promise you'll be careful while you're investigating this story."

"I promise," she said.

"Liz, I've got to go," Todd said regretfully. "I'll call you again in a couple of days. I love you."

"I love you, too," she whispered before hanging up.

Elizabeth expected her twin to tease her, but Jessica wasn't at all interested in talking about Todd. "*Now* can I tell you what *I* went through today?" she demanded.

Elizabeth laughed. "Sorry I made you hold

your tongue for so long. I thought you'd be tired of talking after a day on the switchboard!"

"This is serious, Liz," Jessica pleaded.

Jessica's haunted expression gripped Elizabeth's attention. "Jess, what's the matter?" she asked worriedly. "And by the way, where is everybody?"

"Mom and Dad are at a reception at the museum, and Steven and Adam went bowling. I've been scared to death hanging around here all by myself. And you can't tell me anymore that I don't have anything to be afraid of. Listen to this!"

Jessica launched into an account of Greenback and Rock's most recent, and most frightening, conversation. Elizabeth's eyes widened as the import of her sister's words sank into her brain. "Jess, do you know what this means?"

Jessica nodded. "There's no doubt about it now. The delivery-service messages are definitely connected to Tracy's murder. And there's a bad cop leaking information to the drug ring!"

"A bad cop." Elizabeth's blood ran cold. "Jessica, if there's a bad cop, then he or she knows about your involvement in the case, and what you told Detective Jason about eavesdropping on the phone at work. And if *that* person knows, the rest of the drug ring knows, too. Greenback and Rock *were* talking about you!"

Jessica was very pale. "Liz, what am I going to do?" she whispered.

Before Elizabeth could even begin considering how to respond to Jessica's desperate question, the telephone rang, its bell sounding loud in the quiet house. Elizabeth picked it up, expecting Lila or her own best friend, Enid.

Instead, a strange man's voice met her ears. "If I had my way, you'd be shark bait by now, Jessica Wakefield," he rasped. "From now on, you'd better keep your mouth, eyes, and ears shut, or I'll shut 'em for you."

"Who is this?" Elizabeth cried. But the man just hung up.

Elizabeth stood for a long moment, her whole body trembling. Then she turned to face her twin.

"Who . . . who was that?" Jessica asked anxiously.

"It was a man." Despite Elizabeth's effort to sound calm, her voice shook. "He thought I was you—he actually used your name. And he said you'd better keep quiet, or . . . or . . ." Elizabeth couldn't bring herself to repeat the exact threat. "Or else."

Her eyes wide with fear, Jessica put a hand to her throat, as if she could already feel herself being strangled the way Tracy had been. "It *has* been them," Jessica croaked. "All those hang-up phone calls. They've been watching me the whole time!"

As if on cue, the phone rang yet again. Jessica screamed; Elizabeth jumped.

"Don't answer it," Jessica begged when Elizabeth reached for the receiver.

Elizabeth was afraid to answer it, and afraid not to. She picked up the phone. "Hello?" she said weakly.

It was a man again, but to her relief, the voice was different and he identified himself immediately. "It's Detective Jason," Elizabeth whispered, passing the phone to her sister.

The ensuing conversation sounded harmless enough to Elizabeth. Detective Jason just seemed to be checking in with Jessica. But when the call ended, Jessica was shaking.

"What did he want?" Elizabeth asked. "Has something happened?"

"He didn't want anything," Jessica replied. "He asked if I was all right, and whether I'd overheard anything else before I left work, even though when he called me at the office this afternoon I told him I wasn't using the same phone anymore and so I couldn't eavesdrop. And then he reminded me that I shouldn't talk to anyone about the case and I should tell him everything I see and hear, and oh, Liz!" Jessica threw herself into her twin's arms. "He's *too* nice and concerned. He calls me all the time! It's like *he's* keeping tabs on me, too. I just know he's the bad cop!"

As Elizabeth watched, Jessica yanked the phone cord right out of the wall. "I never want to talk on the phone again for as long as I live!" Jessica cried.

Elizabeth bit her lip. Jessica, who had spent half her waking hours on the telephone! But Elizabeth did not laugh at her sister. The situation wasn't even remotely funny anymore.

"I understand why you didn't want to tell the police about that phone call last night, but I still think we should tell Mom and Dad," Elizabeth said to Jessica as they drove to work the next day. "They should know that you've been threatened outright like that."

Jessica had made Elizabeth promise not to tell their parents about the anonymous phone call, or about the conversation she had overheard that had revealed the existence of a crooked police officer and the fact that the drug ring was aware of Jessica's interference. Jessica shook her head emphatically. "No, they probably wouldn't let me leave the house. I don't want to be treated like a prisoner."

Elizabeth sighed. "OK. But if we get any more calls like that, I'm telling them."

"Maybe there won't be any more calls," Jessica said hopefully. "Maybe they'll catch the criminals today!"

"Let's hope so." Elizabeth pulled the Jeep over in front of Caster's Bakery. "I could go for a donut. How about you?"

"Let's get a couple of dozen to take to the office," Jessica suggested.

In the bakery, Jessica breathed in the delicious

smells while Elizabeth gave her order and then fumbled in her purse for her wallet. As she did so a brochure of some sort fell onto the floor.

Jessica bent to pick it up. " 'Luxury living at Pacific Heights,' " she read, her curiosity piqued. "What's this?"

"It's a new condominium development up the coast. Seth is moving into a unit there," Elizabeth explained. "Yesterday evening on our way back from San Diego we took a detour so he could show it to me."

They walked back to the Jeep with two big bags of donuts. As Elizabeth started the Jeep Jessica selected a plump jelly donut. Munching on it, she examined the brochure. "This looks like a pretty ritzy place," she observed, studying the photographs. "There's a swimming pool and tennis courts and even a health club! How can Seth afford to live there on a reporter's salary?"

Elizabeth shrugged. "I don't know. I hadn't really thought about it."

"Hmm." Jessica finished her donut and licked the sugar from her fingers. "Pacific Heights . . . maybe being a reporter is a more lucrative career than I thought!"

"Maybe," Elizabeth agreed.

Jessica continued to wonder. So Seth was living in a deluxe new condo. *And the condo's not the only thing, either,* she realized, gazing thoughtfully out the window. Seth had also just purchased an expensive new sports car, even though his other car was only a couple of years old. Jessica recalled their recent lunch at Chez Sam. The prices were steep and Seth had not let them pay a penny. He seemed to be throwing around a lot of money these days. Where was it coming from?

All at once, a terrible suspicion stole into Jessica's mind. She shot a panic-stricken glance at Elizabeth but she didn't say anything aloud.

Jessica knew one way people could make a lot of money fast, but it wasn't legal . . . and it sometimes led to murder.

At the *News* office that morning, Jessica made a surprising discovery. The phone system was back to normal. When she dialed in to her own phone line from the switchboard in between other calls to the paper, she didn't hear a thing out of the ordinary.

Jessica called the telephone company. "We've finally straightened out the interference caused by the construction next door," a service representative confirmed. "You shouldn't have any more problems."

"They fixed the phones," Jessica informed Elizabeth a short while later.

"Are you disappointed or relieved?" Elizabeth asked.

Jessica shrugged. "Well, now I'll never know whether Maggie stays with her husband, Frank, or elopes with Craig, the country club pro. And

I'll never know if Junior works up the nerve to tell his mother not to try to run his life."

"And you won't be hearing any more of Greenback's delivery messages, either," Elizabeth reminded her.

"Right," said Jessica. "So from now on, I won't know *anything*. I'm not a threat to them anymore. Maybe now they'll leave me alone," she concluded hopefully.

The phone buzzed. "Good morning, the *News*, may I help you?" Jessica asked. "This one's for you, Liz," she said, transferring the call to her sister's extension.

While Elizabeth talked on the phone, Jessica sorted through a big pile of envelopes on her desk. In addition to taking all the calls, as temporary receptionist she was also responsible for distributing the mail.

Jessica took hold of the sorted stack, preparing to make the delivery rounds. At the same moment, Elizabeth slammed down the phone and jumped up from her chair. "Where are you going?" Jessica called as Elizabeth dashed for the door.

"That was someone who might have a tip about Tracy!" Elizabeth explained excitedly. "See you in a while!"

Mail in hand, Jessica followed her sister. Passing Elizabeth's desk, Jessica spotted the Pacific Heights "luxury living" brochure. *I'll take this, too*, she decided. Instead of thinking the worst, she might as well just *ask* Seth about the money. He was sure to offer an explanation that would clear her mind.

Seth's door was open a crack. Jessica knocked and peeked through before pushing it open. She saw Seth hang up the phone. Then he just sat there for a moment, drumming his fingers on the desk, a preoccupied expression on his handsome face.

Jessica rapped lightly on the door. "Mail call," she announced, walking over to drop a couple of envelopes into his in box.

Seth looked up, distracted. "Uh, thanks, Jess."

"Here's something else." As she handed him the condominium brochure Jessica decided not to beat around the bush. "Liz told me about your great new condo. New car, new apartment— you're really living in the fast lane these days, Seth. How do you swing it on the kind of money you make here?"

Seth raised his eyebrows. "You're either going to make a good reporter, Jessica, or a good private detective," he said. "Talk about getting right to the heart of the matter. What a question!"

"Well, if it's such a good question, why don't you answer it?" she persisted.

Seth laughed. "Let's just say we smart guys tend to have more than one iron in the fire," he said, evading her questions.

"That's all you're going to tell me?"

Seth gave her a smug smile. "That's all, Ms. Nosy."

Jessica lingered, waiting for Seth to change his mind and volunteer some more tangible information. Instead, he put his hand on the telephone, a clear signal that he considered their conversation to be over.

Jessica turned to leave. At that moment, the telex machine on Seth's work table started to print out a news report. Jessica froze in her tracks. That sharp mechanical chatter sounded very familiar. Then she realized why. It was just like the background noise she had heard in the last phone call between Greenback and Rock!

Before Seth could see her expression, Jessica hurried from his office. Back in her own office, she closed the door behind her and leaned against it, her heart pounding. Just yesterday she had been laughing over the possibility that Seth might be Junior. Now it occurred to Jessica that her line may have been crossed with Seth's after all. Only Seth wasn't Junior, he was . . .

Jessica collapsed into her chair, her mind racing. The puzzle pieces were all falling into place, and she did not like the picture they formed. Seth having so much money, and making so many phone calls lately . . .

Jessica tried to fight down her terror. But she couldn't. It washed over her in waves, just as the ocean waves had washed over the strangled body of Tracy Fox.

Just when she thought she might be safe again, she was in more danger than ever. Because if her hunch was correct, the man who had been making the delivery phone calls, the man who had arranged to have Tracy Fox killed, the man who was keeping an eye on the "nosy girl"—and hadn't Seth just called her Ms. Nosy?—had been sitting a few yards away from her the entire time. Jessica was convinced. *Seth Miller was Greenback!*

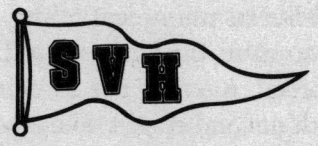

Ten

Elizabeth drove toward Big Mesa as fast as the law would allow. She was excited by the phone call she had received at the newsroom. Someone had seen Tracy's photograph in the paper that morning and responded to their plea for information!

It was very intriguing. The man had identified himself over the phone only as Old Riley. When she had asked him to come to the office of the *News*, he had told her he didn't have a car. So Elizabeth had offered to travel to his house. Old Riley had given the north end of Moon Beach in nearby Big Mesa as his address.

As well as being excited, Elizabeth was also a bit apprehensive about going alone to meet Old

Riley. The anonymous threat to Jessica was still uppermost in her mind. What if this was some kind of setup? *Maybe I should've waited for Seth to get off the phone instead of just taking off by myself,* Elizabeth thought, biting her lip. But his door had been closed, leading her to believe that the call was personal and might take a while.

I'll be all right, Elizabeth told herself. *The beach is a public place, after all. I'll just be careful to stay within sight of other people.*

After parking the Jeep in the Moon Beach municipal lot, Elizabeth crossed the grassy dunes to the beach. Putting her hand to her forehead, she squinted up the shore, past the clusters of sunbathers and swimmers. At the far end of the crescent of white sand, she saw a solitary figure. Old Riley, Elizabeth guessed.

Notebook in hand, she walked quickly up the beach. As she neared the lone man she saw that he was standing at an easel, busily sketching the seascape. There was absolutely nothing shady or suspicious about the appearance of the weather-beaten old man dressed in sunbleached overalls and a straw hat. *He's an artist!* Elizabeth realized, her nervousness evaporating.

She approached quietly. For a moment she looked over the old man's shoulder, admiring the drawing. She thought he hadn't noticed her. But then he spoke.

"I've been trying for years, but I'll never capture the skittery movement of those little pipers," he remarked, his voice gruff. He gestured with one gnarled hand at the tiny birds darting along the water's edge. "I can't freeze such a free and joyful motion."

"I think you've done a good job, Mr. Riley," Elizabeth said, walking around to his side.

He looked up at her. His light gray eyes sparkled in his wrinkled brown face. He tore the sheet from the pad and held it out to Elizabeth. "It's yours. Ms. Wakefield, is it?"

"That's right," Elizabeth confirmed. "But you can call me Elizabeth." She had brought a copy of that day's *Sweet Valley News* with her. Now she showed Old Riley the front page. "Mr. Riley, you called me because you recognized the girl in this picture, Tracy Fox. Were you friends with her?"

Old Riley shook his head. "I never spoke with her. But I saw her walking on the beach a number of times this summer. She looked lonely, and aimless, as if she didn't have anyplace to go. A few times she came close enough for me to get a good look at her. I sketched her once."

Old Riley flipped through his sketch pad. He stopped at a drawing of a young girl standing at the water's edge and gazing out over the water. The girl was in profile, but Elizabeth could see a distinct resemblance to Tracy Fox's yearbook photograph.

"Did she come here every day?" Elizabeth asked.

"Not every day. A couple of times a week for about a month."

"And she was always alone?"

"No. Once a man met her here. They talked for a few minutes. Then he left."

Elizabeth fought to control her excitement. A man! Maybe it was Rock, the man Jessica believed had murdered Tracy. Or maybe it had even been Greenback himself, the drug ring's apparent leader!

"Would you describe the man for me?" Elizabeth requested eagerly. Opening her notebook, she stood poised to write down the old man's words.

But instead of answering, Old Riley took up his own pencil. With quick, sure motions, he sketched a figure on the pad. Elizabeth watched, holding her breath.

In a flash, the sketch was completed. Old Riley stepped back so Elizabeth could take a good look at it.

Elizabeth studied the face, which was in profile, as Old Riley's drawing of Tracy had been. The man was young, with dark hair and a straight nose and strong chin. There was something vaguely familiar about the likeness. *Have I seen this man before?* Elizabeth wondered, her pulse racing. *Do I know him?*

"Mr. Riley, have you gone to the police with this information?" Elizabeth asked. "It might be helpful to their investigation."

Old Riley rubbed his stubbled chin. "You know, I did call the Sweet Valley police station, the very first time I read about her picture in the paper. I told the officer—Detective Jason was his name—about what I'd seen. Thought maybe they'd send someone to see me to get an official statement. But no one even called me back.

Elizabeth thought it was distinctly odd that the police wouldn't have followed up on a potentially important lead. *Detective Jason again*, she thought. *What's he up to? Maybe Jessica is right to be suspicious of him!*

"May I take this?" Elizabeth asked Old Riley, indicating the sketch.

"Of course." He ripped the drawing from the pad. "I wish I could do more. That poor young girl. She would walk quietly, watching the birds. She didn't look like she was capable of harming anyone. It's just a terrible shame that anyone should have harmed her."

"I agree with you," Elizabeth said softly. "Thank you for your help, Mr. Riley."

She held out her hand. He shook it. "Come back and see me again if I can do anything more," he offered.

"I will," Elizabeth promised.

Turning, she trudged back down the beach the way she had come, carrying the two rolled-up drawings. Before returning to the parking lot, she glanced over her shoulder. In the distance, she could see Old Riley and his easel, alone on the empty stretch of sand.

Jessica could hardly wait for Elizabeth to get back to the office so she could share her suspicions about Seth. Finally, at about noon, Elizabeth returned from her interview.

"Liz, we've got to talk," Jessica said urgently.

"About what?" Elizabeth asked. "Oh, hi, Seth!"

Seth had trailed Elizabeth into the twins' office. At the sight of him, Jessica jumped.

"Hi, guys," Seth greeted them. "Want to walk with me to the Box Tree Café to grab a bite?"

"That sounds—" Elizabeth began.

"Sorry," Jessica cut in bluntly. "We've got other plans." Jessica grabbed her twin's arm and hauled her past Seth and across the newsroom to the door.

As soon as the elevator door shut behind them, Elizabeth turned to her twin and placed her hands on her hips. "Jessica, why were you so rude to Seth like that?"

"I'll tell you in a minute," Jessica whispered, glancing distrustfully at the other occupants of the elevator. "Let's get out of the building first!"

Outside the Western Building, Jessica dragged Elizabeth down the sidewalk. At a safe distance, she sat down on a bench.

Elizabeth sat next to her. "OK, Jess," she said

sharply. "Now do you want to tell me what your problem is?"

Jessica spoke slowly and somberly, giving her words the maximum dramatic effect. "Seth Miller is Greenback!" Jessica concluded her story.

But instead of congratulating her twin for her brilliant deduction, Elizabeth burst out laughing. "Seth is Greenback? Then I'm Jack the Ripper. Jess, I think you've finally lost it. Being the temporary receptionist must have scrambled your brains."

"Elizabeth, this is serious. I have evidence." Jessica presented the case in her most businesslike manner. "First, there's the fact that Greenback works in the Western Building. And he told Rock that he had his eye on me. That could mean he actually works with me, at the newspaper! Then there's the fact that Seth has a lot more money than he could possibly make as a reporter. He bought an expensive new sports car, is moving into a luxury condo, and drops cash wherever he goes, like the other day when he took us to Chez Sam. And when I asked him where all the money was coming from—"

"You *asked* him?"

"I was investigating my hunch, like a good reporter," Jessica explained. "When I asked him, he just gave me this sly smile and basically threw the question right back at me, refusing to give me a straight answer. 'We smart guys tend to have more than one iron in the fire' was all he'd say."

"That doesn't sound so incriminating to me," Elizabeth commented. "And I don't blame him for brushing you off. His finances are none of your business!"

"Well, you should've been there when I confronted him," Jessica said. "You should've seen the expression on his face. He was bragging about being so smart. He *looked* like someone who thinks he's above the law. He looked like a drug dealer!"

Elizabeth giggled. "I'll bet."

Jessica scowled. "Laugh if you want, but that's not the only evidence. Add to that the fact that Seth has been making a lot of phone calls lately, and with his door closed, too. You can't deny it, Liz!"

"No, I can't deny it," Elizabeth agreed calmly. "Seth has a lot of money and he makes a lot of phone calls. But Jessica, that doesn't mean that he's the head of a drug ring! This is simply the most outrageous story I've ever heard you come up with. Jess, you know Seth almost as well as I do. He is completely trustworthy, and kind, and honest. He would never engage in illegal activity and he would *never* do anything that brought harm to other people. How could you even think such a thing?"

Jessica shook her head. It was unbelievable how badly Seth had bamboozled Elizabeth into thinking he was Mr. Nice Guy. "The evidence all points to the same conclusion, Liz."

"The evidence all points to the same conclusion because you've let your imagination run completely away with you!" Elizabeth retorted. "Get a grip, Jessica. The next thing I know, you'll be thinking *I'm* involved in the drug ring, too!"

Jessica sighed. "I didn't want to believe it either," she said grimly. "But people aren't always who you think they are."

"You're right." Elizabeth tapped Jessica on the head with the rolled-up sheets of paper she was holding. "Take you, for example. I thought you were my twin sister, Jessica Wakefield. But you're really a raving lunatic!"

"What is that?" Jessica indicated the papers.

"They're drawings. The man who called me with information about Tracy gave them to me, and I didn't even have a chance to put them down on my desk just now before you pulled me back out the door!"

Jessica snatched the sheets from Elizabeth and unrolled them. The sketch of the man was on top. "Who is this?"

"Some guy who was talking to Tracy at the beach once," Elizabeth explained. "I suppose he could have been any random acquaintance. He wasn't necessarily a drug contact."

Jessica stared at the sketch. "Seth! It looks exactly like Seth," she pointed out triumphantly.

"Seth or any one of hundreds of guys with dark hair," Elizabeth scoffed. "Would you cut this out, Jessica?"

"Not until you take a good look at this drawing and tell me it doesn't resemble Seth in the least," Jessica bargained.

"OK." Elizabeth took the drawing. And as she examined it Jessica saw a puzzled frown crease her twin's forehead.

"Well?" Jessica demanded.

"There is a slight resemblance," Elizabeth admitted.

"I told you so!"

"A *slight* resemblance," Elizabeth repeated. "But I'm sure it's just a coincidence. I simply refuse to believe that Seth Miller is involved with this crime in any way. And I'll prove it to you!"

She jumped to her feet and began striding back toward the Western Building. "Where are you going?" Jessica asked, trotting after her. "Don't you want to get some lunch?"

"I'm going to talk to Seth about this," Elizabeth replied. "I'll buy something to eat at the coffee shop later."

"I don't think you should talk to him, and I don't think you should show him the drawing, either," Jessica said as she followed her sister through the revolving door into the Western Building's lobby. "I may already have blown it by asking him about the money. We don't want him to know that we've figured out—"

Jessica cut her sentence short as she walked right into Elizabeth. Without warning, her twin had stopped dead in her tracks. "What's the matter, Liz?" Jessica squeaked.

"I just remembered where I saw Tracy Fox!" Elizabeth answered excitedly.

Jessica's heart jumped into her throat. "Where?"

Elizabeth pointed toward the elevator bank. "Right here!"

Jessica gasped. "Here? In the Western Building?"

Elizabeth nodded. "It's all coming back to me now," she said quickly. "It was a week or so ago—maybe more. I was coming back in from lunch. And I saw a girl waiting in the reception area. She was standing near the elevator, and I noticed her because she looked really nervous. She was fidgeting, shifting her weight from one foot to the other, fussing with her hair. And her hair looked like it hadn't been combed in a while. Her clothes were kind of on the rumpled side, too."

"Wow. Tracy Fox was here in the Western Building—and not long before she died!" Jessica shivered. She felt as if the dead girl were still there, watching them.

"I wish I'd said something to her. But I was in a hurry to get back to the office and finish a story I was working on with Anita, so I didn't give her a second thought. Jessica, what do you think she was doing here?"

"I bet she was going to see somebody here at the newspaper," Jessica guessed.

"That's it!" Elizabeth cried. "She was going to blow the drug ring's cover!"

"She didn't blow its cover, though," Jessica reminded her sister in a low voice. "More likely she was here to pick up some more cocaine from *you-know-who*."

Elizabeth glared at Jessica. "If only there was some way to find out who she came to see. It would prove that Seth isn't involved in any of this! And it would provide a clue for the police about who *did* kill Tracy Fox."

"I know!" Jessica exclaimed. "The visitors' register! No one who's not an employee is allowed into the building without signing in. Tracy would have written down the name of the person she was visiting. All we have to do is look in the book!"

"You're a genius, Jess," Elizabeth praised. "When you're not being a nut case, that is. There's only one snag."

Simultaneously, both girls looked in the direction of the Western Building's receptionist. Jessica grimaced. Ms. LePage was about the nosiest and most unfriendly person on earth. Though she always had a movie-star magazine open on her desk, she still managed not to miss a thing that went on in the lobby. On more than one occasion, Ms. LePage had hollered at Jessica for not showing her employee ID badge promptly enough.

"There's just no way we're going to be able to

get a look at the visitors' register without her knowing what we're after and broadcasting it all over the building," Elizabeth said grimly.

Jessica nodded. Then her eyes lit up with sudden inspiration. "I know!" Leaning over, she whispered her plan in Elizabeth's ear.

"Are you ready?" Jessica asked Elizabeth as they stood outside the Western Building on Friday morning. "You're going to have to be fast."

Elizabeth nodded. "I'm ready."

"So am I." Jessica's eyes sparkled. Elizabeth knew her twin loved to pull a good stunt. "So let's go for it!"

Elizabeth pushed through the revolving door. Casually, she strolled across the lobby. And then she couldn't resist peeking over her shoulder. She looked just in time to see Jessica stop dead in her tracks right inside the door. "Omigod!" Jessica cried at the top of her lungs, pointing back out toward the street. "I think I just saw Michael Jackson!"

As Elizabeth watched, Ms. LePage practically vaulted over her desk. "Where?" she shrieked, abandoning her post to race to Jessica's side as fast as her high heels would carry her.

"In that car over there," Jessica replied excitedly. "Hurry or you'll miss him!"

As Ms. LePage clattered out the door Elizabeth dashed over to the reception desk. The visitors' register was resting on top, open to the current date. Rapidly, Elizabeth leafed backward through the pages. A week . . . ten days . . . There it was! Tracy Fox's name!

Tracy had signed in at one-thirty, Elizabeth noted rapidly, and out again at one-forty—a very short visit. And the sign-out time was written in a different handwriting from the rest of the information. This was puzzling, but Elizabeth didn't dwell on it. Because even more surprising was the name scrawled in the "Person Visiting" column. Elizabeth didn't want to believe the evidence of her own eyes, but the name was recorded there, plain as day. Seth Miller!

At that moment, Ms. LePage burst back into the lobby. "I saw Michael Jackson, too," Elizabeth heard her gush to Jessica, who had waited by the door. "Thanks, honey. That was the most thrilling moment of my life!"

With a hurried gesture, Elizabeth returned the register to its original position and stepped away from the desk. She met Jessica by the elevator. Jessica was grinning from ear to ear. "Was that the perfect scheme or what? Did you hear her yell? She actually thinks she saw Michael Jackson!"

Then Jessica must have noticed Elizabeth's distressed expression, because her smile faded. "What did you find out, Liz?"

Elizabeth didn't want to tell Jessica what she had discovered, but she knew she had no choice.

"I found Tracy's name in the book," she said. "She was here for only ten minutes."

"Who did she come to see?" Jessica asked eagerly.

Elizabeth choked out the words. "She came to see Seth."

The sisters stared at each other. The devastating fact was now undeniable. Seth Miller had been involved with Tracy Fox in some way. In her life . . . and possibly in her death.

Eleven

"I told you so," Jessica chided her twin as they rode up to the fifth floor in the empty elevator. "I never trusted Seth. He always seemed a little strange to me."

"That's baloney," Elizabeth retorted. "You had a big crush on him at first."

Jessica folded her arms across her chest. "It's no use, Liz. You'd better face the facts. Seth is a drug dealer, and probably a murderer!"

"You can't assume that just because of what Tracy wrote in the register," Elizabeth said, wanting very much to give Seth the benefit of the doubt. She pointed out the more puzzling aspects of the case. "Why did her visit last only ten minutes? What could they possibly have discussed in that time? Besides, if Tracy had come up to Seth's office, wouldn't other people have noticed her? Maybe she never even left the lobby. Whatever her reason for coming to the Western Building, maybe she just changed her mind and left. That would explain why the sign-out time was in someone else's handwriting—Ms. LePage's, probably."

"It would take only ten minutes to make an exchange," Jessica countered. "And she wouldn't have needed to go all the way up to the newsroom. Naturally she and Seth would have met someplace else in the building, somewhere less public. Like the stairwell."

Elizabeth shook her head. Jessica could argue all day, but Elizabeth just couldn't believe such a thing of Seth. He was her friend and colleague; they'd been working closely together all summer. Elizabeth knew how much Seth loved his work. He was a dedicated reporter, a man of integrity and commitment. He could get pretty intense when it came to chasing after a fast-breaking news story, but for the most part he was easygoing and sweet. He simply *couldn't* have a secret life, a criminal identity. He couldn't be caught up in the tangled, deadly web of a drug ring!

"He just couldn't be guilty," Elizabeth declared aloud. "Jess, I know Seth."

"You just *think* you know Seth, Liz, but you really don't," Jessica insisted. "You only met him through this internship. Maybe he showed you his new condo, but you don't really know what his life is like outside of the office, or what his life was like in D.C. before he moved to Sweet Valley. You know only part of Seth Miller. The part he wants you to see. And of course he's going to look and act like an ordinary person most of the time. That's how he pulls it all off!"

"Well, there's one way to resolve this question," Elizabeth declared as the elevator door swished open at the fifth floor. "I'm going straight to Seth's office to ask him about Tracy's visit." Elizabeth stepped determinedly from the elevator.

"Liz, stop!" Grabbing Elizabeth's arm, Jessica yanked her down the hall, away from the office door.

"Jessica, let me go," Elizabeth demanded. "Haven't you ever heard the expression innocent until proven guilty? Seth deserves a chance to explain himself to us before you do something drastic, like have him dragged off to jail in handcuffs!"

"You can't tell him what we know," Jessica argued. "Liz, you have to admit there's something fishy going on around here. No matter what happened that day, Tracy Fox signed in to visit Seth. Seth *knew* her. And yet he never admitted that he knew anything about Tracy or the case. So obviously he's hiding something!"

"OK, he's hiding something," Elizabeth conceded grudgingly. "But it might not be—"

"It doesn't matter what it is," Jessica interrupted. "There's a chance he's innocent of anything really serious, although I personally doubt it." Elizabeth glared at her. "But you have to admit there's also a chance that he's not," Jessica continued. "And if he's not, Liz, it could be very dangerous to let him know we suspect him. I don't think you should say one word to him about this. And don't show him the sketch, either!" She paused thoughtfully. "We can't wait for the police to solve this case. We need to get more evidence—to prove either that Seth's innocent or that he's guilty."

"And how do we do that?"

Jessica's eyes gleamed. Elizabeth knew that look; her twin was hatching another devious scheme. "Tonight after work, I'm going to go through his files," Jessica announced. "I bet I'll find lots of evidence!"

Elizabeth's eyes widened. "Jessica, you can't do that!" she protested.

"Oh no?" Jessica shot her twin a challenging look. "Just try and stop me!"

"I really don't feel comfortable doing this," Elizabeth said to Jessica as they parked the Jeep on the first level of the garage next to the Western Building at ten o'clock that evening.

"Well, I've made up my mind and I'm going in," Jessica declared. "You didn't have to come with me, you know."

"I know." Elizabeth's forehead creased in a worried frown. "But I didn't like the thought of you in the office all by yourself at night. It might be dangerous. Oh, Jess, let's just go home!"

"No way." Opening her door, Jessica jumped out of the Jeep. "Wait here if you want!"

Jessica anticipated that Elizabeth would find the thought of waiting alone in the garage even less appealing than going upstairs to snoop through Seth's files. Sure enough, Elizabeth stepped out of the Jeep and hurried after her sister.

The only entrance to the Western Building that was open after hours was through the garage on the ground floor. As the sisters walked toward the door Jessica noted how empty and quiet the garage was. There were only a few scattered cars. Jessica wondered if Seth's—Greenback's—car was still there, parked on one of the other levels.

"Have you—have you ever worked at the office this late?" Jessica asked Elizabeth, not wanting to admit that suddenly she was a little nervous herself.

"No. I've stayed until seven or eight, but never ten. *No* one stays that late. The layout editors usually put the paper to bed by eight."

The twins rode the elevator to the fifth floor without speaking. The hall outside the news office was dim; through the full-length plate glass panes, they could see that the office itself was pitch black. *Good. No one else is here*, Jessica thought.

She took her office key and unlocked the glass door. On tiptoe, she and Elizabeth slipped into the dark office.

For a moment they just stood there. Jessica's heart was beating like a jackhammer; she could hear Elizabeth's breath coming quickly, too. There was something very creepy about the usually bright and bustling newsroom being so dark and still.

But it was too late to turn back. Since they were there, they might as well do what they had come to do. Stepping soundlessly, Jessica led the way to Seth's office. "Should we turn on a light?" Elizabeth whispered.

"No." Jessica felt her way over to Seth's file cabinets. "Someone could be watching the building. Besides, my eyes are adjusting. I can see well enough by the lights from the street."

Elizabeth hung back by the door. "Just hurry, OK?"

Obediently, Jessica opened the top drawer of the cabinet and began flipping rapidly through what seemed like hundreds of hanging files. She didn't know exactly what she was looking for. Would there be a folder titled "Greenback"? "Cocaine"? Jessica stifled a nervous giggle at the thought that Seth would advertise his guilt in such a fashion.

"Hurry up, Jess!" Elizabeth urged. "I think we should get out of here."

"I'm hurrying," Jessica muttered. She pulled

out a folder labeled "Fox Murder" and shuffled through its contents. There was nothing out of the ordinary in there, just various scraps of papers on which Seth had scribbled uninteresting notes about the case. Jessica grabbed a couple of other folders at random, hoping to stumble by chance on the file that held the key to Seth's criminal connections.

No such luck. With a frustrated sigh, Jessica started stuffing the files back in the cabinet.

"This is crazy," Elizabeth hissed.

"Seth hasn't left any evidence around," Jessica was forced to admit. "But then," she rationalized, "what good criminal would?"

Elizabeth stepped forward to seize her twin's arm. "Come on, Jess. Let's go!"

She pulled Jessica away from the file cabinets. At that moment, they heard a muffled sound from the far end of the dark newsroom. The sound was repeated. It was coming closer.

Footsteps! Jessica clutched Elizabeth's sleeve. The twins stared at each other, their eyes glazed with terror. Someone was walking toward them in the dark!

Jessica knew they should hide. But even though her life depended on it, she couldn't move a muscle. She was paralyzed with fright. Elizabeth, too, had frozen as stiff as a marble statue.

And the slow, measured footsteps were getting louder, nearer. *It's the murderer*, Jessica thought, biting back a scream. *It's Seth, coming to strangle us!*

Jessica squeezed her eyes shut. She didn't want to see Seth's murderous face looming in front of her through the gloom.

Suddenly, a light went on in the newsroom. Jessica opened her eyes. A tall, broad-shouldered man with dark hair stood in the doorway of Seth's office.

Jessica nearly fainted with relief. "Bill!" she exclaimed, putting a hand on her heart. She had never been so glad to see anybody in her entire life.

"Working late, I see," Bill said with an easy smile.

Jessica smiled back, but she was tongue-tied. What explanation could she offer for why she and Elizabeth were snooping around Seth's office in the dark? And she was still holding one of Seth's stupid folders!

Fortunately, Elizabeth was thinking fast. "I remembered I needed something for one of the stories Seth and I are working on," she said glibly, indicating the file in Jessica's hand. "Jessica came with me to get it."

"I'm just picking up some papers myself," Bill remarked. "I'll see you two tomorrow. Don't work too hard."

"Oh, we won't." Jessica recovered enough to flash him her most engaging smile.

Bill stepped away from the door. The twins

prepared to make their escape from the newspaper office.

"Oh, one thing, Jess." Jessica turned to face him again. Bill reached into the pocket of his leather jacket. "I was going to put this back on your desk. I picked it up by accident this afternoon when I was retrieving some of my dictation tapes. Then I saw it didn't have one of my usual labels on it. Is it yours?"

He handed a small cassette to Jessica. She gulped as she recognized it. It was the tape on which she had recorded the last few delivery-service messages, including the conversation about the bad cop!

"Thanks, it is mine," she said, wondering if Bill had listened to the tape. But his expression as he waved goodbye to the twins and stepped into his office was nonchalant. Clearly he had no idea what the cassette contained. "Well, see ya!" Jessica called after him.

The twins ran at top speed down the stairs. "That sure was a lucky break!" Jessica gasped as Elizabeth started the Jeep's engine. "I thought for sure it was Greenback coming to get us."

"I just hope we didn't look too suspicious," said Elizabeth.

"Not a chance," Jessica replied. "You were very cool. That story was perfect. Besides, Bill's got more important things to think about."

Elizabeth turned onto Main Street and cruised

through a few green lights. Soon they entered a residential area.

"But was I ever stupid to leave that tape lying around!" Jessica groaned. "What if *Seth* had picked it up? He would've known I was on to him! Speaking of which, too bad we didn't come up with any more evidence against—I mean, evidence one way or the other. Don't forget to sneak that file back in his—ouch!" Jessica yelped. Where are you going, Liz?"

Elizabeth had made a sharp, unexpected turn, throwing Jessica against the car door. Now, instead of answering, Elizabeth made another sudden turn. When she spoke, her voice was grim. "Don't look now, but I think we're being followed."

Jessica twisted in her seat. She saw what Elizabeth must have noticed in the rearview mirror; a sleek, dark car trailing a short distance behind the Jeep.

At the sight of the shadowy figure behind the wheel, Jessica's heart beat fast with a mixture of fear and excitement. "Are they really following us?"

"They've been behind us since town," Elizabeth confirmed. "And they stayed with me even after those two sudden turns."

"Step on it, Liz," Jessica urged.

Elizabeth took a deep breath. "OK. Here goes!"

She stepped on the gas. The Jeep surged forward, racing through the quiet neighborhood. The dark car also gunned its engine, staying right behind them. "I can't outrun them," Elizabeth cried. "Hold on, Jess!"

Jessica braced herself. Elizabeth slammed on the brakes. Tires squealing, she pulled into a driveway, then immediately backed up onto the street to head back in the opposite direction.

The other car had also braked. Now the two cars passed each other. Elizabeth raised a hand to shield her face from the gaze of the other driver, but Jessica craned her neck trying to get a look.

"It's just one person," she told Elizabeth. "A man, with light hair and a hat—a baseball cap, I think. But he turned his face away." Jessica swiveled to see if the man would also turn around in a driveway. But instead of following their lead, he continued on in the opposite direction.

Jessica watched until the car disappeared in the distance. Then she sank back in her seat. "He's gone."

Elizabeth relaxed her viselike grip on the steering wheel. But when she lifted a hand to push a strand of hair off her forehead, Jessica could see that she was shaking. "You were right, Jess. There *was* someone watching the building," Elizabeth said. "Watching *us.*"

Suddenly, Jessica remembered the incident a few days earlier when a light-haired man in dark glasses and a baseball cap had appeared to be shadowing her during her lunch hour. "I wonder if that was the same guy I thought was following me the other day?" She shuddered. "Oh no, Liz, maybe that was Rock! Why do you suppose he stopped trailing us?"

"Maybe he was just trying to scare us," Elizabeth said.

"Maybe."

The twins drove the rest of the way home without any problems. But both were badly shaken. As Elizabeth parked the Jeep outside their home, Jessica knew her sister had to be thinking the same thing she was: what if next time their pursuer—Rock?—didn't give up so easily?

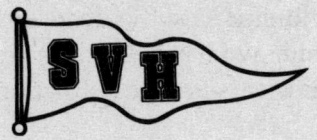

Twelve

It was a sunny day, and Jessica and Lila were at the beach. Jessica wanted to sit on her beach towel and read fashion magazines, but Lila tugged at her hand, pulling her to her feet. "Come on, Jess," she urged. "Let's go see what's washed up down at the other end of the beach!"

Unwillingly, Jessica followed Lila to the spot where a crowd of people had gathered. Oddly enough, the people didn't have on bathing suits but were dressed for work; Jessica recognized many *Sweet Valley News* staffers in the crowd.

Lila pushed her way through them in order to stand next to the crumpled thing lying on the sand. "She's dead!" she called to Jessica.

Jessica joined her friend reluctantly. She forced

herself to look down. A man with dark hair was bending over the body; his hands around the girl's cold white throat. He was strangling her! And then Jessica saw the dead girl's face. It was a mirror image of her own.

"No!" Jessica screamed, turning to run. "No! Don't let it be me!"

"Jessica!" Lila shouted after her. "Jessica!"

Someone was shaking her. "Jessica. Jessica, wake up!"

"No," Jessica mumbled, still half asleep. "Don't let it be me!"

"Jessica, wake up. You're having a bad dream!"

Slowly, Jessica opened her eyes. By the light of the moon streaming through her bedroom window, she could see Elizabeth bending over her. When Elizabeth saw that her sister was finally awake, she relaxed her grip on Jessica's arm. "You had a bad dream," Elizabeth repeated softly.

Jessica sat up. "I sure did. Did I wake up the whole house?"

"No, just me."

Remembering the dream, Jessica shivered. She sank back against the pillows, pulling the covers up to her chin. "I'm scared, Liz," she whispered. "I'm scared that I'm going to be next. That *my* body's going to wash up on the beach one of these days."

"I'm scared, too," Elizabeth confessed. "After

that man followed us tonight it really hit home. We're in this thing deep."

"We have to do something. We have to get help. We have to tell someone about Seth!"

Elizabeth shook her head vehemently. "Jessica, it's not Seth. There's someone out there and he knows about us. *They* know about us. But Seth's not one of them. I still feel sure about that."

"Well, I still feel sure that he *is* one of them," Jessica countered. "Liz, we're in danger. You know it as well as I do. I thought they'd leave me alone, since I can't eavesdrop on their conversations anymore. But they must think I know too much because of what I already overheard. Tonight, we got away because they *let* us get away. But next time . . ." Jessica clutched her sister's arm fearfully. "Next time they won't let us get away," she finished. "Next time my nightmare will come true. Someone will find our bodies at Castle Cove!"

"All right then." Elizabeth reached for the phone on Jessica's night table. "Let's call the police right now."

"No. We can't! The bad cop," Jessica reminded her.

"That's right." Elizabeth sighed.

"Thank goodness it's the weekend," said Jessica. "I'm going to stay right here in bed the entire time!"

"And miss Winston's party tomorrow night?"

"I'm not leaving this house," Jessica affirmed.

"But on Monday we'll have to go back to the office," Elizabeth reminded her.

Jessica was already dreading Monday. She'd have to be in the same building as Seth Miller!

Elizabeth observed the distress on her twin's face. "Jess, promise me you'll give me a few more days before you tell anyone your suspicions about Seth," she begged. "Just give me until Monday. I know I can find a way to clear Seth, and then we'll have him on our side. We can tell him what's been going on, and he can help us figure out what to do next."

"OK," Jessica agreed grudgingly. "But just until Monday!"

I promised Liz, Jessica reminded herself at work late Monday morning. *I promised Liz I wouldn't tell anyone about Seth yet.*

But she had made that promise only so Elizabeth would have an opportunity to clear Seth. And what were the chances that she would be able to do that? Zero, zilch, Jessica believed. Because Seth Miller was guilty with a capital G. No two ways about it.

And there was something else Jessica was sure of. She couldn't live with this terror any longer. Every time the phone rang, her heart just about stopped. If someone standing behind her coughed, she hit the ceiling. She was scared of her own shadow. The only thing that kept her from having a complete nervous breakdown was the fact that Seth was out of the office for the morning.

She needed to go to *somebody* with her information about Seth. But who? Jessica drummed her fingernails on the top of her desk, glad that Elizabeth was off with Anita researching a story on summer days in Sweet Valley. Elizabeth would guess in a second what she was contemplating!

Just then, Jessica's restless gaze came to rest on a memo in her in box. It was from Bill, requesting her to hunt up some things in the newspaper morgue. Bill . . . Jessica's eyes lit up. Of course! She could explain everything to Bill! He was so smart and cool and level-headed; she could talk to him about anything, and he was bound to know what to do. And after all, as her boss and Seth's boss, shouldn't Bill be informed that one of his employees was running a drug ring from the newspaper office?

Without a moment's hesitation, Jessica pushed back her chair and marched straight to Bill's office. His door was ajar, and she knocked on it lightly. "It's just me, Jessica," she called out. "Can I talk to you for a minute?"

"Sure, come on in."

Bill was taking a fax from the machine on his work table as she entered. He waved her into a chair. "What's up, Jess? If it's about leaving work early today to play in the tennis round robin with your friend, you already have my permission."

"No, it's something else." Jessica took a deep breath. "I need your advice, Bill. I need your help. It's about Tracy Fox's murder and the drug ring. I think I know who's behind it all!"

Bill's dark eyebrows shot up. "You do?"

Jessica nodded. "See, there was something I didn't tell you, back when the telephone system was all screwed up. My line was getting crossed with a bunch of others in the building. I could listen to other people's conversations. And I think one of the people I overheard was the leader of the drug ring. He was always making these bizarre phone calls, in code I think, and at first I thought he ran a shipping company or delivery service. But then I heard him plotting to murder someone!"

"Tracy Fox?"

Jessica nodded again. "He never mentioned her name, but when her body was found a few days later, and she was carrying a packet of cocaine, I knew Greenback was responsible."

"Greenback, eh?" Bill sat down at his desk. He propped his elbows on the arms of his chair, rested his chin on his tented fingers, and contemplated Jessica with narrowed eyes. "And you say you know who he is?"

"You're never going to believe this," Jessica warned him, praying, of course, that he *would* believe her. "The head of the drug ring is Seth Miller!"

"Seth!" Bill's blue eyes popped wide open. "You're kidding!"

"I know it sounds crazy, but just listen." Quickly, Jessica listed her reasons for suspecting Seth. "I didn't want to believe it either at first, but it all adds up," she concluded. "Elizabeth actually saw Tracy downstairs in the lobby a day or two before she died. And we found out by checking the visitors' register that Tracy was here to see Seth! That's the real reason Liz and I were in the office Friday night, when we ran into you. We wanted to see if we could find more evidence."

"I think you have plenty of evidence already," Bill declared.

"You do?"

"I do," he said firmly. "It adds up, just as you said."

A wave of relief washed over Jessica. Bill believed her! "It does, doesn't it?"

"I'm afraid so." Bill shook his head. "I liked Seth at the beginning. But I completely agree with you that he's been acting strangely lately. I've noticed the same things you did, Jessica. The frequent, secretive phone calls—and his lifestyle is definitely far beyond what most newspaper reporters can afford. I know how much money he's making here and it's not an awful lot! But I didn't put it all together." Bill looked at Jessica, his eyes warm with admiration. "I've got to hand it to you, Jessica. You were very clever to check the visitors' register. You're quite a sleuth."

Jessica glowed at his praise. Finally, she was going to get the credit she deserved for cracking the case! "Do you think we should confront Seth?" she asked.

Bill considered. "No," he said at last. "I think it would be best to take the whole story to the police. You probably should be going now if you want to get to the country club on time, but I'll be working late. Why don't you meet me back here tonight? We can go to the station and make a statement together."

Jessica hesitated. She hadn't gotten a chance to tell Bill about her experience with the police, and her reason for not wanting to talk to them: her discovery that there was a crooked cop on the force in league with the drug ring.

But suddenly, Jessica recalled another aspect of that final conversation between Rock and Greenback. Rock had warned Greenback about an undercover police officer who had been assigned to investigate the drug ring.

In a flash, the final piece of the puzzle fell into place. *The undercover officer—it must be Bill!* Jessica deduced. His relatively recent arrival at the newspaper, his vague answer that time she had asked him about his previous job . . . it all tied in perfectly. What a stroke of luck that she had thought to come to him with her dilemma!

I can leave everything to Bill, Jessica thought, so relieved she practically fell off her chair. Soon

Seth, Rock, and the rest would be behind bars. The nightmare would be over.

Bill was still waiting for her answer. "I think that's a great idea!" Jessica told him.

He smiled. "Good. Like I said, I've got a lot of work to catch up on, but I should be done by nine. I'll see you back here then, OK?"

As she waltzed back to her desk Jessica felt secure for the first time in ages. To make her day perfect, it was already noon and she had Bill's permission to leave for the day! When Lila had first invited Jessica to be her guest for a teen tennis round robin and garden party at the country club, Jessica had been lukewarm at the prospect. How could she *play* at a time like this? But now, she was suddenly full of energy. She couldn't wait to get onto the court! *Bill's an undercover agent, and we're going to turn Seth in,* Jessica exulted. *I don't have to be afraid anymore. I can live my life again!*

Grabbing her jacket and shoulder bag, Jessica breezed out of the office. Downstairs in the lobby, she was surprised to see Ben Donovan talking to Ms. LePage, the receptionist.

Ben glanced in her direction. Jessica tossed him a casual wave.

He crossed the lobby to join her. "Jessica, hi. How are you today?"

"I'm fantastic," she replied, flashing him her most dazzling smile. "Couldn't be better!"

"I'm glad to hear that," Ben said sincerely. "Jessica, are you by any chance free for dinner tonight?"

Jessica almost burst out laughing. Not long ago, she would have swooned over Ben's invitation. That was before she knew what a bore he was. Still, he *was* amazingly good-looking. She might have gone out with him if she didn't have anything better to do that night.

But she did have something better to do. She was going to bust the Sweet Valley drug ring!

"Sorry." Jessica flashed Ben another breathtaking smile—just a little something for the poor guy to remember her by. "I have other plans. See you around!"

Thirteen

"Do you think you have everything you need to draft the article, Liz?" Anita asked after lunch on Monday.

"I'm all set," Elizabeth told her. "As soon as I'm through, I'll run it by you for comments."

"Great. Thanks for all your help."

"Thank you for giving me a chance to draft an article on my own!" Elizabeth replied.

Anita disappeared into the newsroom, leaving Elizabeth alone in her office. Elizabeth looked at Jessica's unoccupied desk. *That's right*, Elizabeth remembered. *Jess left work early to play in a tennis tournament with Lila*. Elizabeth was almost relieved that Jessica wasn't around. She had been worried that her twin would panic and act on her suspicions about Seth. Elizabeth hoped that an afternoon at the club with Lila would distract Jessica from her fears.

But Elizabeth knew the distraction would be only temporary. And Elizabeth agreed with her twin—their situation was dangerous and it was time to take action. There wasn't a moment to waste. Before Jessica blew the whistle on Seth, Elizabeth had to talk to him and get to the bottom of his involvement with Tracy Fox.

Jessica doesn't want me to do this, Elizabeth thought as she walked purposefully to Seth's office. But no matter what Jessica might think about the potential danger of letting Seth know they were on to him, Seth was still Elizabeth's friend. She owed it to him to find out his side of the story.

Seth was typing rapidly on his computer keyboard as Elizabeth stepped into his office. When he saw her, he hit the save key and cleared the screen. "Hey, Liz. Are you looking for some work to do?"

"Sure, if you have some for me. But that's not what I came to see you about."

He raised his eyebrows at her serious tone. "Is something wrong, Liz?"

Elizabeth pulled up a chair. She sat down and looked steadily across the desk at Seth. "I found something out about Tracy Fox," she told him.

"You did? Is it newsworthy?"

Elizabeth was glad that he seemed eager and

curious, not at all like a man who had something to hide. But she knew she had to be cautious. The real test would come when she confronted Seth with the evidence of the Western Building's visitors' register.

"Yes, it is newsworthy." Elizabeth pointed to a bulletin board on the wall of Seth's office. The front-page article with Tracy Fox's photo was pinned to it. "Seth, when I first saw that picture of Tracy, I recognized her. I realized I'd seen her somewhere."

"You're kidding!"

Elizabeth nodded. "It's true. It came to me late last week that I had seen Tracy right here in the lobby, only a day or two before she died. I assumed that she was waiting to see someone who works in the building, and so Jessica helped me look through the visitors' register. We found Tracy's name." Elizabeth paused, wishing she didn't have to say what came next. "And Seth, she'd written that the person she was visiting was *you*."

Elizabeth's words had a profound effect on Seth. His jaw dropped. "Me?"

"Seth, I've got to know the truth," Elizabeth pleaded. "What was your relationship to her? Why didn't you tell the police that she came to see you before she died? Why didn't you tell *me*?"

Seth shook his head. "Elizabeth, I didn't have *any* relationship to Tracy. Not until I started writing about her after her death, that is. I never met her. She *never* visited me."

"But she wrote your name in the register," Elizabeth persisted. She couldn't bear to think that Seth was lying to her. "She came here to see you. She couldn't have been a stranger to you, Seth. Please don't deny it!"

"Liz, I swear, I never met her," Seth insisted. "You've got to believe me. I would never lie to you, and certainly not about anything like this."

"Then why would she have written your name in the visitors' book?" Elizabeth demanded. "How do you explain that?"

Seth wrinkled his forehead. "Liz, I have absolutely no idea—" Suddenly his brow cleared. "Wait a minute!"

Elizabeth sat forward, gripping the armrests of her chair. "What, Seth?"

"A couple of weeks ago I got a phone call. I'd almost forgotten about it! Some investigative reporter I am," he said grimly. "I never would have made the connection!"

"What connection? What phone call?"

"A girl called me," Seth elaborated. "She wouldn't give me her name, but she sounded young—and nervous. She said she wanted to talk to me right away about a very important story. I told her to come over as soon as she could. She called me in the morning. It was . . ." He racked his brain. "It was July twenty-first or twenty-second. But she never showed up."

"It must have been Tracy Fox!" Elizabeth exclaimed. "The twenty-second was the day I saw her, the day she signed the visitors' register. She *did* show up, Seth. I bet she was planning to meet with you in order to expose the drug ring!"

"But I never saw her," Seth said.

"No, for some reason she didn't stick around long enough to talk to you," Elizabeth agreed. "According to the register, she stayed in the building for only ten minutes. And someone else—Ms. LePage, I imagine—signed her out. She probably got cold feet and just left."

"Cold feet," Seth said thoughtfully. "Or she was scared off by something . . . or someone."

Elizabeth's head spun as she pondered this latest twist on the Tracy Fox story. For a moment, she and Seth looked at each other in silence. "Seth, I'm sorry about accusing you," Elizabeth said at last. "I just wish Jessica were here to hear this. She's ready to turn you over to the police!"

"It's OK. I don't blame you guys for wondering what I was up to. But you can believe me," Seth said earnestly, "when I say I had nothing to do with Tracy Fox's death." Then he lowered his voice to a whisper. "But I think someone else at the newspaper did."

Elizabeth caught her breath sharply. "Who?"

"I can't tell you—yet," Seth replied. "I'm waiting for some information to be faxed to me at home today. I couldn't risk having it sent here. Come by my place tonight, Liz," he urged. "I'll explain everything then."

Elizabeth hesitated. She was incredibly curious, and there was nothing in the world she wanted more than to be able to believe whole-heartedly in Seth's innocence—and to help him apprehend the real criminals! But what if Jessica was right? Seth could be lying. This could be some sort of trap.

She was tempted to risk it, to trust Seth. But common sense told Elizabeth that she had to protect herself. She wanted to believe Seth so much—too much, maybe. But there were still a lot of things she had not accounted for.

"Let's . . . let's meet someplace public," Elizabeth suggested haltingly.

A shadow flickered across Seth's eyes. She could see that he was hurt that she still doubted him. But he nodded, and when he spoke, his tone told Elizabeth that he understood her feelings. "OK. The Box Tree Café at nine o'clock?"

"I'll be there," she promised.

On the way home from work, Elizabeth stopped at the market to buy some fresh produce to make a salad for dinner. She filled her basket with leaf lettuce, ripe tomatoes, green and yellow peppers, and a big bunch of carrots, and then got in the checkout line.

"Liz, is that you?"

Elizabeth turned. Standing behind her in the line was Rose, the former receptionist at the *News*.

"Rose, hello!" Elizabeth greeted the other

woman warmly. "It's nice to see you. We miss you at the newspaper. Jessica especially! She's been answering the phones since you left," she explained. "How do you like your new job?"

Rose frowned. "What new job?" she said, her voice cracking. "I've been looking ever since Bill fired me, but I still haven't found anything."

"Fired?" Elizabeth was shocked. *Hadn't Bill said that Rose quit in order to take a better position somewhere else?*

"After all those years . . ." Rose shook her head. "I guess loyalty doesn't mean anything these days. It's hard, Liz. Harry and I just aren't managing too well on only one salary."

"You'll find something," Elizabeth reassured her. The cashier rang up her order and Elizabeth removed a few bills from her wallet. Before leaving the store, she turned to Rose once more. "Good luck, Rose."

"Thanks, Elizabeth. I'll need it!"

Walking back to the Jeep, Elizabeth pondered what Rose had told her. Why on earth would Bill have fired Rose? As far as Elizabeth could tell, she had always been an exemplary receptionist. The newsroom certainly hadn't been running as smoothly as it had when she was working there.

And if Bill fired Rose, why did he say she'd quit to take another job? Elizabeth wondered as she drove the rest of the way home. *But maybe he didn't say that—maybe I only remember it that way.* Elizabeth shook her head. So many other things had been going on at the office that for the life of her she could not recall Bill's exact words that morning when he had announced Rose's departure.

Still befuddled, Elizabeth parked the Jeep in the driveway and entered the house. As she deposited the grocery bag on the kitchen counter, a piece of notebook paper caught her eye.

The sheet was covered with Jessica's distinctive scrawl. *Liz*, Jessica had written, *I've got the situation under control. I'm going to the police with Bill Anderson at nine tonight to tell them about Seth. I'll fill you in when I get home!*

"Oh, no!" Elizabeth groaned. She should have known Jessica wouldn't be able to stick to her promise to keep her mouth shut! *Seth will be pretty annoyed when the police show up later tonight with a warrant for his arrest*, she thought grimly.

But maybe it wasn't too late to stop Jessica and Bill from taking such a drastic step. Elizabeth flipped through the phone book and found the number for the Sweet Valley Country Club. She dialed it rapidly. "Yes, I'm trying to get in touch with two people who were playing in the tennis round robin," she explained to the employee who came on the line. "Would you please page Lila Fowler and Jessica Wakefield?"

Elizabeth waited impatiently. "I'm sorry," the employee informed her at last. "The party ended a short time ago and your friends didn't respond to my page. They must have left the club."

"Thanks." Elizabeth hung up and dialed

another number. But the Fowlers' housekeeper told her that the girls weren't at Lila's house, either.

Elizabeth cursed her luck. Obviously, Jessica and Lila had gone out someplace after the tennis party. They could be anywhere in Sweet Valley—the Dairi Burger, Guido's Pizza Palace, the Valley Cinema, the mall. There was no point in trying to track them down, Elizabeth realized in frustration. She would only waste a lot of time and energy.

No, she would just have to hope that the evidence Seth had turned up, the evidence he was going to share with Elizabeth that evening, would be sufficient for him to clear himself. If not, it was very likely that Seth Miller would be spending the night in jail.

"Do you want me to wait for you?" Lila asked as she pulled the Triumph over in front of the Western Building a few minutes before nine o'clock that evening.

"No, that's OK. Bill will take me home," Jessica told her.

Lila scrutinized her friend. "There's something you're not telling me, Jess," she accused. Then Lila's brown eyes popped wide open. "Are you and Bill *dating?*"

Jessica burst out laughing. "No, Li. We're not dating! We're just working on a project together, and we didn't manage to finish it this morning. I figured that since he let me take the afternoon off to play with you, the least I could do was come back to the office for a few minutes tonight."

"You are *such* a poor liar," Lila remarked. "And you've been acting very weird ever since that day we went to Castle Cove and saw the dead body. I'm tempted to keep driving and not let you out of the car until you tell me what's really going on. But I suppose I can get the story tomorrow."

"You'll get the story tomorrow," Jessica promised. She was already imagining the newspaper headline: "Reporter Seth Miller Busted for Drug Dealing and Murder!"

Jessica stepped out onto the curb and waved goodbye as Lila drove off. Then she hurried through the parking garage to the elevator bank.

The Western Building was dark and quiet, just as it had been the night that she and Elizabeth sneaked in to look at Seth's files. But tonight it didn't seem so creepy, and Jessica wasn't the least bit nervous. Just knowing that Bill, an undercover police officer, was waiting upstairs for her made all the difference.

The door to the newspaper office on the fifth floor was unlocked. Jessica let herself in. At the far end of the dark newsroom, she could see a sliver of light coming from Bill's office.

Jessica quickly made her way across the newsroom, weaving among the desks and chairs. Bill's door was ajar, and she pushed it open without knocking. Bill was seated, hunched over his cluttered desk. Jessica's sudden entrance seemed to startle him. He sat up abruptly and pushed something off to the side of his desk among a pile of papers.

"Sorry for bursting in like that," Jessica apologized. "I guess I'm a few minutes early. I didn't mean to make you jump!"

"It's OK. I'm just a little . . . distracted." Bill ran a hand rapidly through his dark hair and flashed her a fast smile. "A great story idea just hit me," he explained, "and I thought I'd scribble down some notes."

Bill is really an amazing guy, Jessica thought as she sat on the edge of a chair across from him. A brilliant newspaper editor *and* an undercover agent! She couldn't help noticing that he seemed a little nervous tonight, though, a little jittery. Then it occurred to her. Of course, they were probably in for quite a scene at the police station. Maybe there would be a big confrontation between Bill, the undercover agent, and the bad cop—maybe even a shootout! *Bill's probably just worried about dragging me into the middle of it all,* Jessica concluded. *I'd better tell him my suspicions about Detective Jason. Then he'll be more prepared.*

"Well, I'm ready," she said. "Let's go! And on the way over to the station, I'll give you the details about what happened after I went to the police the first time."

Bill sat back in his chair and clasped his hands behind his head. "What's the rush?" he asked.

Jessica blinked, puzzled by Bill's suddenly nonchalant attitude. "Well, there's no rush, I guess. I just figured we shouldn't waste any time. I mean, this is pretty crucial. A lot of lives could be at stake. Mine, for example!"

To her surprise, Bill laughed, a strange, high-pitched giggle that sent a shiver down Jessica's spine. "Your life, Jessica, is in very good hands," he assured her. He laughed again. "And the police aren't going anywhere."

Jessica was confused. Bill's attitude struck her as out of character, and completely inappropriate to the situation. *What's with him?* she wondered. He was usually so nice. But tonight there was something very odd about him.

Jessica had the feeling that she didn't know the man sitting across the desk from her. He was like a stranger, and a very unattractive one. For the first time since she had entered his office, she took a closer look at Bill's usually neat and handsome appearance. His necktie was loose and his hair rumpled; the blue eyes that usually made her swoon were watery and bloodshot.

Maybe he's sick, she thought, dropping her eyes so he would not think she was staring.

Then she noticed something on the corner of Bill's desk, something she had not spotted when she first sat down. It was a little plastic vial containing some kind of white powder. There was a tiny spoon attached to it.

For a moment, Jessica stared at the vial without comprehension. Then the color drained slowly from her face. She had never actually seen any, but she had heard about it. She knew what the vial contained. Cocaine!

That was what Bill was doing when I came in! That's why he looks like this, why he's acting like this. Jessica went numb with shock. It seemed unbelievable, but the evidence was right there in plain view. Bill had not been writing down story ideas when Jessica burst into his office and caught him off guard. He had been snorting cocaine.

Jessica edged back her chair, her wide eyes darting from the vial of cocaine to Bill's face. He was smiling at her. If he had seen her observe the vial, he didn't seem to care.

I've made a mistake—a big mistake, Jessica realized. She didn't know who Bill Anderson was, but one thing was for certain: he was *not* an undercover agent, and he wasn't about to go with her to the police station to make a statement about Seth's involvement with the drug ring. He was probably buying drugs from Seth himself!

Her heart pounding with fright, Jessica jumped to her feet. She had to get out of there, and fast!

Bill's smile faded and his lips tightened in a hard, white line. "Where are you going?" he snapped.

"I—I just remembered," Jessica stammered, inching backward in the direction of the door. "I have to . . . to meet someone. We can take care of this tomorrow, right?" Taking another step back, she reached behind her and felt for the doorjamb.

"You're not going anywhere!" Bill replied. Springing from his chair, he lunged for her.

With a scream, Jessica whirled and ran from Bill's office. As she fled she hit the light switch on the wall. His office light went out and the newsroom was instantly swamped by the blackness that Jessica knew was her only hope for escape.

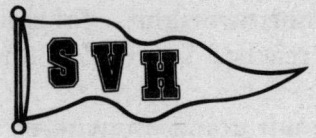

Fourteen

Elizabeth parked the Jeep halfway down the block from the Box Tree Café in downtown Sweet Valley. As she walked to the restaurant she spotted Seth's new Mazda.

He's already here, she thought. In just a few minutes he would show her the evidence he claimed to possess, evidence that would clear him from suspicion and plant that suspicion on someone else—someone else who worked at the newspaper!

Her palms tingling with nervous excitement, Elizabeth entered the café. She glimpsed Seth at a secluded corner table and in a moment was seated across from him. "Did you get the information you were waiting for?" she asked.

A large folder rested on the table in front of Seth. He placed both hands on top of it and leaned toward Elizabeth. "I've got everything I need now," he replied, his eyes glittering. "It's all here in black and white. Liz, you're never going to believe this!"

"Believe what?" she demanded. "Seth, would you please tell me what's going on?"

Seth flipped open the folder and removed a stack of glossy sheets smeared with tiny print. "These are faxes from various newspapers around the country," he explained, handing them over for Elizabeth's inspection.

Elizabeth examined the faxes eagerly. They were copies of newspaper articles. She read some of the headlines out loud. " 'Teen-aged Girl Shot in Execution-Style Killing.' 'Youth's Death Linked to Drug Cadre.' 'Drug Ring Leader Evades Murder Investigation.' " She looked up at Seth, her forehead wrinkled. "These sound like horrible crimes. But what do they have to do with *our* crime, with Tracy Fox's murder? For that matter, what do they have to do with one another? There are five newspaper articles here and each one is from a different city. Plus, none of the dates is all that recent." Elizabeth tapped a fax from a Miami paper. "This murder took place four years ago!"

"They don't *appear* to be related in any way," Seth agreed. "Unfortunately, drug-related deaths are a dime a dozen in big cities these days. But they *do* add up to something, Liz. There *is* a common denominator. These murders are like a trail of footprints. I followed the trail, and guess what I've discovered."

Elizabeth shook her head. "I can't guess. What?"

"None of these cases has been solved. The killer or killers got away in every instance. And also in each instance, someone we both know lived in the city at the same time that the crime was committed."

A chill ran up Elizabeth's spine. Her fingers tightened on the fax she was holding. "Who?" she asked in a strained voice.

Seth's eyes bored into hers with a burning intensity. "Bill Anderson," he whispered.

"What?"

"I'm certain of it," Seth asserted. "Not that I ever expected in a million years that this is what I would find when I started investigating Tracy Fox's murder. As you know, I did a computer search and I came up with a list of literally hundreds of drug-related murders. But when I started weeding through the cases, looking at those with characteristics similar to those of Tracy's case, I ended up with a sort of trail. And as I looked at the cities—Denver, Miami, Montreal, Las Vegas—something clicked in my brain. They were all places where Bill Anderson had lived before coming to Sweet Valley!"

"He *has* lived in a lot of different cities,"

Elizabeth conceded. "But it could be just an amazing coincidence, Seth. You can't accuse him on the basis of—"

"I made sure it was more than a coincidence," Seth interrupted her. "Take a look at these."

He removed a few more items from the folder. Elizabeth saw that they were police department mug shots. She studied the face in the first one, then gasped. "It's Bill!" she exclaimed.

"It's Bill, all right," Seth confirmed. "His hair was a lighter color, and he had a mustache. And he was using another name. But it's him."

Staring at the mug shots, Elizabeth suddenly remembered Old Riley's sketch. Jessica had been so certain that the picture was of Seth. But now that Elizabeth thought about it, she realized that the young, dark-haired man in the drawing could just as well be Bill Anderson!

Elizabeth was struck speechless. She stared across the table at Seth, trying hard to master her tumultuous thoughts and emotions.

"I'm telling you, Liz, he's got a criminal record a mile long," Seth continued. "Drug possession, assault and battery . . . They never got him for any of the murders, but I'm convinced he's responsible. If he didn't commit them himself, he ordered someone to do it. And every time, he managed to skip town just one step ahead of the law. He'd move to a new place, change his name and his appearance, make some new connections, and set up shop all over again. Liz, he's been running a drug ring out of *our* office!"

Elizabeth nodded. She knew it was true; it fit exactly with what Jessica had overheard on the phone. Only Jessica had concluded that it was Seth she was eavesdropping on, when the whole time it was Bill!

"I believe you," Elizabeth said. "Listen to this!" Quickly, she filled Seth in on the drama of the crossed telephone lines. "Jessica's line was crossed with four or five others in the building, one of which belongs to someone who calls himself Greenback. He made a lot of short calls. They always sounded like delivery instructions. I remember the first one she told me about: 'Red fish up the coast highway to point seven,' " Elizabeth quoted. "I didn't think anything of it at the time. But then Jessica overheard a conversation in which Greenback and an acquaintance talked about how someone's body was soon going to be found floating. The next day, Tracy washed up on the beach. Greenback had ordered his contact, some guy named Rock, to kill her!"

Seth whistled. "Wow. That clinches it!"

"It seems to," Elizabeth agreed. "Jessica even taped a few of the phone calls. You know, they were part of the reason she suspected *you*, Seth. She thought you were Greenback! But I guess all the phone calls you've been making lately were to track down information about Bill."

Seth affirmed this with a nod. "Greenback," he mused. "A code name. Bill Anderson probably isn't even his real name. It looks as if he changes identities as casually as he'd change his shoes. I wonder who he really is."

"He's a monster," Elizabeth said with a shudder. "Seth, why haven't you gone to the police with this?"

"It's the biggest story I've ever worked on, Liz. I didn't want to blow it," he answered. "I wanted to keep my information to myself until I could be sure I was on the right track. The mug shots came just this evening. Now I'm ready to set the police on Bill. Before someone else gets hurt," Seth added.

Before someone else get hurt . . . Suddenly, Elizabeth remembered the note Jessica had left for her on the kitchen counter. *I've got the situation under control*, Jessica had written. *I'm going to the police with Bill Anderson at nine tonight to tell them about Seth.*

Elizabeth clapped one hand over her mouth, her eyes widening with terror. "Oh, no," she whispered. "Seth, I think Jessica is with Bill right now! She left a note at home saying that they were going to the police together tonight in order to turn you in!"

"Bill Anderson wouldn't risk going anywhere near the Sweet Valley police station," Seth said grimly. "And he's not likely to let Jessica go, either."

"Which means . . ."

Elizabeth and Seth shoved back their chairs simultaneously. "We've got to stop her!" Seth declared.

"We've got to stop *him!*" Elizabeth cried.

Panting, Jessica dashed down the hall in the dark, heading in the direction of the elevator. Her skin prickled. At any second she expected to feel Bill's hands on her throat.

Don't panic! she commanded herself, biting back a sob. If she let her fear get the best of her, Bill would catch her. And then . . .

Only one thing was on her side: the pitch darkness of the office. Jessica expected Bill to flood the place with light in order to illuminate her fleeing form. But he didn't hit any of the switches. *He's not turning on the lights because he doesn't want to catch the attention of anybody down on the street—he doesn't want to risk anyone seeing us through the windows,* Jessica deduced. *Because he's going to kill me!*

Her knees weak from terror, Jessica continued to grope her way toward the elevator. Halfway there, she realized her mistake. It was a dead-end route. Bill would expect her to try for the exit. She would be an easy target, waiting for the elevator or running down the well-lit staircase. And even now, Jessica could hear his heavy footsteps close behind her in the dark, getting closer.

Abruptly, she cut to the right. Feeling before her with desperate hands, she scrambled across the large open newsroom. It was like maneuvering blindfolded through an obstacle course of desks and chairs and file cabinets. She couldn't afford a single misstep; her life depended on speed and silence.

If I can just get to my office, Jessica prayed, *I can lock the door and call the police. Please, let me get there.*

At that moment, she stumbled over an electrical cord. She let out a startled gasp, then froze, clapping her hand over her mouth. Her heart was pounding so hard, it sounded like the roar of the ocean in her ears. Had Bill heard her? Was he still behind her? Was that his labored breathing that she heard, or her own? Jessica couldn't tell.

Falling to her hands and knees, she crawled across the floor, winding through the forest of desks. Finally, ahead of her, she saw a doorway. Her office! The room was faintly illuminated by the streetlights far below. *I'm almost there. I'm going to make it!*

Rising to her feet again, she groped her way to the door. In two strides, she was at her desk, fumbling for the telephone. Pressing the receiver to her ear, she peered at the phone, trying to read the numbers on the buttons so she could dial the police emergency number.

Then she realized that there was no dial tone. The line was dead.

Dropping the phone, Jessica dashed to Elizabeth's desk. But when she picked up that receiver, again she was met by silence. Tears streaming down her face, Jessica jiggled the button, desperately trying to get a dial tone. But with no luck.

And then the overhead light in the office suddenly came on, blindingly bright.

Still clutching the phone, Jessica whirled. Bill Anderson was standing in the doorway of her office, another eerie smile on his face.

"I thought you might want to use your telephone," he said, stepping toward her, "so I took the liberty of disconnecting it. You should have learned by now, Jessica—that phone brings you nothing but trouble."

Jessica dropped the receiver. It hit the desk with a clatter. Her heart pounding, she looked around wildly. But there was only one way out of the office—through the door, and Bill was blocking it.

He took another step in her direction. As she watched in horror he reached up to his neck and slipped off his tie. He held the tie in both hands, stretching it taut, as if he was preparing to do to her what Rock had done to Tracy Fox, to wrap it around her neck and pull it tighter and tighter until she couldn't breathe.

"No," Jessica begged as Bill came closer. She backed up against the desk, again searching desperately for a way out.

But Bill continued to walk slowly toward her. Jessica knew there was no way out, just as there had been no way out for Tracy. She was trapped!

Fifteen

After leaping up from the table at the Box Tree Café, Elizabeth sprinted through the dining room with Seth at her heels. She almost tripped over a waiter, and the restaurant's other patrons all turned to stare, but Elizabeth was oblivious to them. Her twin was in mortal danger and helping her was all that mattered.

Reaching the pay phone near the entrance to the café Elizabeth rapidly dialed the police station. "This is Elizabeth Wakefield and I need to report an emergency," she panted. "Please send squad cars to the Western Building right away. My sister is there with Bill Anderson—the person responsible for the murder of Tracy Fox!"

"Whoa, whoa," said the officer who had answered the phone. "What did you say? Bill Anderson? Isn't he an editor at the *Sweet Valley News*?"

"Yes, but he's also a criminal. I have evidence," Elizabeth insisted. "My colleague Seth Miller has evidence for you, but first my sister needs help immediately. Her life is in danger!"

"Now, what exactly leads you to believe her life is in danger?" the officer asked. "If Bill Anderson is so dangerous, what was she doing with him in the first place?"

"She works for him. The two of them arranged to meet. But Jessica didn't realize at the time that he—"

"If they arranged to meet, then she must have a very different opinion of him than you do," the officer pointed out. "We haven't received a call from *her* this evening reporting any threat to her well-being."

"That's because he may have already hurt her. He may be holding her a prisoner!" Elizabeth cried.

"Are you yourself at the Western Building right now, Ms. Wakefield?"

"No," she admitted.

"Have you seen your sister and Mr. Anderson together this evening? Have you actually witnessed any improper behavior on his part, either tonight or at any time in the past?

Did she ask you to report an emergency on her behalf?"

"No, but—"

"Then I'm afraid there *is* no emergency," the officer concluded.

"But . . ." Elizabeth threw Seth a desperate glance.

Seth's eyebrows furrowed in a look of puzzlement. "What's going on?" he whispered. "Why are they putting you off? Who is that?"

"Who am I speaking to?" Elizabeth asked the officer.

"This is Detective Jason," he informed her. "And now, Ms. Wakefield, I think we should clear the line in case a *real* emergency call comes through."

Detective Jason . . . Detective Jason was the officer Jessica had gone to with her information about Tracy's murder! And he was also the officer Old Riley had talked to, the one who had chosen not to follow up on Old Riley's sightings of Tracy Fox at Moon Beach.

Elizabeth remembered Jessica telling her about the telephone conversation during which one of Greenback's cronies indicated that there was someone corrupt on the Sweet Valley force. Jessica had become suspicious of Detective Jason because he was overly solicitous. Now he seemed anything *but* concerned about Jessica's safety. *Maybe he is the bad cop!* Elizabeth thought. That would explain why he didn't consider this situation an emergency. He was protecting Bill, possibly at the expense of Jessica's life!

Quickly, Elizabeth hung up the phone. Whether Detective Jason was the bad cop or not, it certainly looked as if she could not count on any assistance from the police. She and Seth would just have to head over to the Western Building alone. And they had better get there fast. If Detective Jason was the bad cop, he might very well go to the Western Building himself, now that Elizabeth had tipped him off to what might be happening there.

Elizabeth grabbed Seth's arm. "Come on!" she urged, pulling him toward the door. "We've got to handle this on our own. And there's no time to lose!"

Too terrified to scream, Jessica squeezed her eyes shut, waiting to feel Bill's hands on her throat. But he didn't strangle her. Instead, he grabbed her arm roughly and yanked her away from the desk and out of the office.

"Ouch!" Jessica cried as his fingers pinched her flesh.

"Shut up," Bill snapped. "Or I'll treat you to some *real* pain."

He pushed her ahead of him, across the newsroom toward the hall and the elevator. *He's kidnapping me,* Jessica thought. *Maybe he'll hold me for ransom.* Her spirits lifted somewhat. She knew her parents would pay any amount to get her back. But then she thought of what had happened to Tracy Fox. *They're making enough money from the drugs—they wouldn't bother with a ransom note. They'll just get me out of the way somehow.*

A wave of hysteria welled up inside her. Jessica fought it down. She knew that only by thinking clearly could she hope to survive. "Where are we going?" she asked, choking on a sob.

Bill shoved her through the door into the hallway. With one finger, he jabbed the up button on the wall next to the elevator. "We're going to take a little ride," he told her, his voice low. "Up to the roof."

As he spoke Jessica heard a new note in Bill's voice: cold, cruel . . . and familiar. She had heard that sound before, but never in person. Only over the phone.

Suddenly, the full realization hit Jessica. "*You're* Greenback," she whispered, her eyes widening. "You're not just part of the drug ring. You're the one who's been running it, not Seth!"

Bill laughed. The elevator door swished open, and he forced her inside. "You've finally got the story straight," he sneered. "But I really should thank you, Jessica, for pointing out how easy it's going to be to frame Seth for Tracy's murder. And for yours."

Jessica gulped. The elevator began to move. She wished it would rise forever, but she knew that in just a few moments they would reach the top of the seven-story Western Building and she would be alone on the high, dark roof with the ruthless Greenback.

Seth sped the few blocks from the café to the Western Building. Seeing a parking spot, he braked, but Elizabeth couldn't wait for him to back the car into the space. Swinging her door open, she jumped from the car and sprinted toward the Western Building.

She had no idea what she and Seth would do or say when they confronted Bill—if Bill and Jessica were even still in the building. They would have to bluff and tell Bill that the police were on the way. Bill wouldn't risk killing all three of them . . . would he?

It didn't matter to Elizabeth. She didn't care that she was running straight into danger. All she knew was that she had to get to Jessica before . . . before . . .

Suddenly, someone seized Elizabeth's arm. With a startled cry, she whirled and found herself staring up at the young man who had stopped her.

He looked strangely familiar. *It's the guy from the office across the street!* Elizabeth realized an instant later. The guy Jessica had been mooning over, but who had turned out to be a boring accountant: Ben somebody or other.

Before Elizabeth could ask him what he wanted from her, he gripped both her shoulders with his strong hands. "Thank goodness you're safe!" he exclaimed.

Elizabeth twisted out of his grasp. "What do you mean?" she asked.

"I was watching you from my office across the street," Ben explained. "Anderson looked like he was threatening you. I thought he might attack you. I was just rushing over to help. How did you get away?"

Suddenly, Elizabeth realized Ben's mistake. "That was my twin sister you saw, not me!" she cried. "I think she's still in there with him! We've got to help her!"

To her astonishment, Ben whipped something out of his jacket pocket. Elizabeth saw that it was a tiny, hand-held radio. He talked rapidly into it. Then he flashed a badge of some sort at Elizabeth and dashed into the parking garage. "Let's go!" he called to Elizabeth and to Seth, who had now joined them.

Breathless, the three came to a halt at the elevator bank. Ben pointed to the illuminated panel over the elevator door. As they watched, the numbers climbed: fifth floor, sixth, seventh. "They're going all the way to the roof!" Ben shouted.

"He's going to throw her off!" Elizabeth screamed.

"Come on." Ben pulled open the fire door next to the elevator. "We'll take the stairs!"

* * *

As they stepped out of the elevator Bill's fingers tightened on Jessica's arm. "There's no point dragging your feet," he told her, laughing cruelly. "I'm taking you to the edge, Jessica, whether you want to go or not."

The roof of the Western Building was dark and windswept. A strand of hair whipped across Jessica's face. Her thoughts chased themselves in desperate circles. *I could run*, she thought. *I could scream. Maybe someone would hear me from the street below.*

Bill read her mind. "Don't even think of opening that big mouth of yours," he warned. "Or these hands will be around your neck so fast, you won't know what hit you. Just walk."

Jessica took one reluctant step toward the edge of the roof, and then another. Her eyes darted around her, but she could see no place to run to, no place to hide. In front of her was the edge of the roof, with its seven-story drop to the pavement below, and behind her was Bill. He had her cornered.

He can't go through with this, Jessica thought. *He can't be planning to kill me.* She had liked and trusted Bill. Everyone at the *News* had. How could he turn out to be so completely evil?

Slowly, so as not to alarm him, Jessica pivoted so that she was facing Bill. "Why?" she asked him. "Why are you doing this?"

Bill raised his hands, snapping the necktie

taut. Jessica took a step backward. "This is just part of doing business," Bill replied coolly.

"But why are you in this business?" she demanded. "Because one of these days it's going to destroy you, too, Bill."

"No, it's not," he yelled at her. "I control it, it doesn't control me." His once-handsome face was contorted with fury.

Reaching out one hand, Bill yanked Jessica toward him. Then he took something from his pocket—a packet of some sort—and shoved it in the pocket of her jeans jacket. "A parting gift," he told her sarcastically, pushing her backward.

Jessica gasped as she realized what he was doing. He had planted drugs on her so that when her body was found the police would think she had been involved with the drug ring. *It'll look like I was a dealer, maybe even an addict!* she thought desperately.

Bill walked toward her, his strong hands lifted. Jessica began to back up, but not without stealing a panicked look over her shoulder. She was getting nearer and nearer to the edge of the rooftop.

"Yep," Bill said, "you're going to jump, Jessica. And this time there won't be any marks on the body. It'll be a suicide, plain and simple."

"You'll never get away with it," she retorted.

"Oh, I'll get away with it," he said with grotesque confidence. "I've gotten away with it time and again. The trick is having other people do your dirty work for you." He smiled. "But this is going to be a special pleasure. I'm glad to have it all to myself."

Her heart pounding, Jessica shuffled back another few inches. A few more steps, and there would be nothing behind her but empty air.

"You thought you were so smart." Bill's eyes narrowed and his lips curled in a snarl. "Eavesdropping on my conversations and then telling the police." He laughed harshly. "You didn't know Detective Jason was a friend of mine, did you? You know, it didn't have to come to this, Jessica. I thought I'd put an end to your meddling when I fired Rose and unplugged your phone. Jason was making sure your story didn't get anywhere at the station. But you went on spying. I heard what you recorded on that cassette."

Jessica cursed herself again for her carelessness. How could she have left that tape just lying around? It was a stupid thing to do—and now it looked as if it was going to cost her her life!

"I—I never told anyone about that tape," she stammered. "I never told anyone about you. And I won't tell. Just let me—"

"It's too late," Bill replied coldly. "There's just too much at stake to let you nose around anymore. This is big business. You teenaged girls are idiots to think you can play the game, to think you can beat my organization!" His voice dropped to a hiss. "Tracy Fox made the same mistake. She made a few deliveries for us, and then she thought she could double-cross us, blow our cover. And you know what happened to *her*."

Her heart in her throat, Jessica took another small step back. She shuffled closer and closer to the edge, until she put a foot behind her and felt the ledge. With a cry, she froze in that precarious position.

Bill smiled at her. He grasped her shoulders roughly, preparing to push. "Rock wanted to do this," he whispered, putting his face close to hers. "He's been calling you, following you, just itching for the chance to do you in. But why should he have all the fun?"

Tears streaming down her face, Jessica closed her eyes. She could not look at Bill's face for a second longer. She could not die with that picture in her mind. *Elizabeth,* she thought. *Oh, Liz, why didn't you come for me? Why didn't you get me out of this mess, like you have so many times before? Goodbye, Liz. I love you. . . .*

There was a rattle of gravel on the other side of the roof, and the sound of pounding footsteps. Jessica's eyes popped open. Someone else was on the roof!

It was the answer to her prayer. She saw

Elizabeth and Seth and another man running toward her. *Ben Donovan!*

Bill whirled, and Jessica shoved him away from her. As she prepared to run, Bill made another grab for her. But before Bill could get his hands on her, Ben Donovan took a flying leap and tackled him.

With a scream, Jessica dashed to Elizabeth's side. The two sisters hugged, but their eyes were glued to the mortal struggle taking place a few feet away.

Locked in a deadly embrace, Bill and Ben wrestled furiously. The two men rolled over and over; at one moment, it looked as if Ben would overcome Bill, but then Bill would thrust Ben from him and regain the advantage. Seth hovered over them, looking for a chance to help.

Suddenly, Bill managed to shove Ben aside and jump to his feet. Ben leaped up, too. Jessica gasped when she saw how close Ben was to the edge of the roof. All Bill had to do was push him, and Ben would plunge to his death on the hard sidewalk far below.

The twins caught their breath as Bill raised his arm. He lunged at Ben, trying to strike him on the head and knock him off the rooftop. "No!" Jessica shrieked.

Just as Ben ducked to evade the blow, Bill's foot caught on a piece of rooftop rubble and he

tripped. For a moment that seemed to last forever, his body was poised over nothingness.
Then, with a final defiant, blood-curdling shout,
Bill fell over the edge and disappeared from
sight.

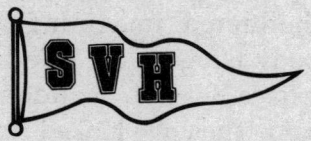

Sixteen

Jessica pressed her face against Elizabeth's shoulder. Elizabeth's arms tightened protectively around her twin. "It's all right," Elizabeth murmured soothingly. "You're safe. It's all over."

Jessica raised her head to look around her. She was still shaking from her ordeal, but now that the danger was past, she couldn't help feeling just a little curious and excited. She stared at Seth and Ben, who stood silhouetted at the edge of the roof, gazing down at the street. The night was a whirl of sirens and headlights as a dozen police cars and an ambulance arrived at the scene. It was just like a movie!

Turning, Seth and Ben walked slowly toward

Jessica and Elizabeth. "He probably didn't survive the fall," Ben said solemnly. "No one could have."

Jessica shuddered, imagining Bill's broken, crumpled body lying on the sidewalk below. "I still can't believe Bill was the leader of the drug ring," she said. Then she looked up at Ben, as it suddenly had occurred to her how odd it was that *he* had shown up at the rescue along with Seth and Elizabeth. "And who are *you*, really? I get the feeling you're not just an accountant who works across the street!"

Ben gave her a crooked smile. Taking something from his pocket, he showed it to her. It was a wallet containing a badge and ID card. "I'm an undercover police officer," he explained. "I've been working on this case for a couple of weeks."

"*You're* the undercover cop?" Jessica couldn't believe how completely backward she had gotten everything. She was too embarrassed to admit that she had thought Bill himself, who had turned out to be the criminal, was the undercover policeman. *And not only that—I thought Seth was a drug kingpin, and Ben Donovan, undercover agent, just a boring business type!*

Ben nodded. "I knew the drug ring was operating out of the Western Building," he continued, "but I needed firm evidence of Bill Anderson's involvement. We were just about ready to close in on him when he tried to close in on *you*."

Jessica crossed her arms across her chest. "I guess I'm pretty lucky you guys came along when you did. A lot luckier than Tracy Fox."

"I saw Tracy rushing out of the Western Building not long before her death," Ben said. "Bill had entered the lobby only a few moments before. From what I could find in the visitors' register, I figured that Tracy was planning to talk to Seth. She probably wanted to come clean and give her story to the paper. She obviously didn't know her drug connection worked at the *News!* She must have seen Bill and gotten scared. And he saw *her* and ordered her to be killed."

Seth shook his head. "Poor kid." He told Ben about the anonymous call he had received from the girl with the big story, the girl who had never shown up. "She made a serious mistake, getting into drugs," Seth said. "But then she must have decided she didn't want to be a victim. She must have realized she was on the wrong track."

"By the time she tried to get off that track, though, it was too late," Elizabeth said sadly.

Up until now, Jessica had not spent that much time thinking about Tracy Fox and what her life must have been like. She had been more interested in trying to figure out Greenback's identity;

Elizabeth was the one who had gotten caught up in Tracy's story. But now, having come so close to death herself, Jessica had a new sympathy and sorrow for the murdered girl. She could imagine Tracy's aloneness, her fear. She had been a runaway, cut off from her family and friends. In Tracy's final moment, there had been no one to come to her rescue.

"My head is still spinning," Elizabeth said. "I can't believe all this was going on right under our noses! What will happen to the drug ring now that Bill Anderson is gone?" she asked Ben.

"The operation won't be able to survive without him," Ben predicted. "He was its mastermind. We have a number of leads that will enable us to arrest the other dealers—those who haven't left the state already, that is. Including the man we believe murdered Tracy, Kevin Stone."

"Stone," Jessica mused. Then her eyes lit up. "Over the phone, Greenback called him Rock!"

"Over the phone?" Ben looked at her quizzically. "Greenback and Rock? What are you talking about?"

"Greenback and Rock are Bill Anderson and Kevin Stone," Jessica said. "I told the police all about the conversations I overheard while my phone line was crossed with some other lines in the building. Somebody who called himself Greenback was running what seemed to be a delivery service, only it turned out to be Bill running his drug dealing organization."

Ben frowned. "Who did you speak to at the station?"

"Detective Jason," Jessica answered.

Quickly, Ben radioed to the squad cars, which were now heading back to the station. "Detain Detective Jason for questioning regarding his involvement with Bill Anderson," Ben barked. "I repeat, do not let Jason leave the precinct."

"So he *was* the bad cop!" Jessica whispered excitedly to Elizabeth.

Elizabeth nodded. "I knew it when I tried to call him tonight to get help for you and he wouldn't cooperate," she whispered back.

"We knew one of the officers was passing along information to the dealers, but until now we weren't sure which one," Ben said grimly. "Jason never told anyone else in the department about the information you gave him, Jessica. Clearly he was suppressing it to protect his partners."

Jessica nodded. "He told me not to talk to anyone else about what I knew. He wanted to be my only contact. He said it was for my own safety, and because the investigation was top secret."

"There was no way you could have known he wasn't trustworthy when his own colleagues hadn't caught on to him yet!" Ben exclaimed. "I'm just sorry I didn't realize your predicament,

Jessica. When you held up the note with your name and number in the window, I jumped at the chance to get acquainted with a *News* employee . . . and a pretty girl," he added, smiling. "I thought maybe I'd learn something about Anderson's behavior. But when we talked that first afternoon, I had no idea you were keeping such a dangerous secret."

"I almost told you at one point, when I felt like I needed some advice," Jessica confessed. "But I had no idea what kind of secret *you* were keeping, either!"

"You probably did the right thing, given the situation," Ben assured her.

"I did a lot of wrong things, too, though," Jessica said, with another apologetic look at Seth. "Like agreeing to meet Bill here tonight—alone. It just never occurred to me that . . . I mean, he seemed like such a great guy. He was so smart and creative." *And gorgeous,* she thought.

"Sometimes it's hard to understand what drives a person to criminal activity," Ben told her. "Bill squandered a lot of his own personal talents, that much is for sure. And if he'd lived, he would have spent the rest of his years in jail for destroying other people's lives as well as his own."

If he'd lived . . . Jessica shivered. She would never see Bill Anderson—those compelling blue eyes, that charming smile—again. And never again would she hear Greenback's murderous voice.

"Greenback is gone," she said out loud.

"Greenback," Elizabeth mused. "It's a code name, like Rock for Stone. Bill, as in dollar bill."

"That's right," said Ben. "I'm sure all the people Jessica overheard on the phone were using code names. It's part of conducting an illegal business such as drug dealing."

"Coyote," Jessica said suddenly, remembering the very first message she had overheard. "Coyote was the name of a young woman. Do you think it could have been Tracy Fox?"

She and Elizabeth looked into each other's eyes. It made Jessica sad to think that she had once heard the dead girl's voice. If only Tracy had never gotten involved with such horrible people! When Bill and Jessica had faced off on the rooftop, Bill had called it a game. But if it was a game, it was a deadly one, in which a single wrong move could cost you your life. A game that everybody who played was bound to lose sooner or later.

Elizabeth put her arm around her sister's shoulders. Slowly, the four of them walked back across the dark rooftop to the door that led to the elevator and the stairwell.

"I know it's late, but I'd like you all to come with me to the station," Ben requested when they reached street level. "I need to get formal statements from you."

"Let me just grab something from my car," Seth said.

A minute later, Elizabeth and Jessica were settled in the back seat of Ben's unmarked police car, on their way to the station. Up front, Seth was telling Ben about the results of his own investigation into Bill's past. Ben whistled as Seth showed him the file full of newspaper articles and mug shots. Clearly, the Sweet Valley police department had focused on Bill's current criminal activities in the Sweet Valley area, never suspecting that he might have such a long and deadly cross-country history.

Jessica was surprised by what Seth was saying. But most of his words did not sink very far into her brain. As they left the Western Building behind it suddenly hit her how close she had just come to losing her life.

Jessica turned to her twin, tears streaming down her face. "Liz, I was so scared. I was so scared that I was never going to see you or Mom or Dad or Steven again."

Elizabeth threw her arms around Jessica, her own eyes bright with tears. She hugged her sister fiercely. "I'll always be there when you need me, Jess," she promised.

Jessica hugged Elizabeth back. Slowly, a feeling of security returned to her. It was like waking up after a black, stormy night to a sunny southern California morning. The nightmare was over.

At the police station, Jessica and Elizabeth phoned their parents. Then they took turns giving detailed statements to the police about the evening's events. Finally, Seth turned over his file on Bill Anderson to Ben Donovan.

"Don't you need this for your newspaper story?" Ben asked. "After all, you cracked this angle of the case. You should get a head start on the rest of the media in breaking it."

Seth grinned. "I've got photocopies of everything at home," he told Ben. "I'll beat everyone to press with this story. And I'll take credit for it, don't worry!"

A squad car drove Seth and the twins back to the Western Building, where Seth's car was parked. "Seth, will you drop us off at my car?" Elizabeth asked. "It's still over at the restaurant."

"I'll drop you off at home," Seth said. "The Jeep'll be fine parked there overnight. And I won't rest easy unless I see you two right to your door."

"Thanks," Elizabeth said. She couldn't deny that she would be glad to have Seth's company for a while longer. It hadn't been too many nights before that she and Jessica had driven home late from the Western Building and been followed by one of Bill's cronies, probably Rock himself.

Elizabeth climbed into the passenger seat and Jessica jumped in the back. As Seth pulled away from the curb Jessica leaned forward. "There's just one thing I don't understand, Seth," she said. "Where *did* you get all the money to buy this car and to move into the new condo?"

Seth smiled sheepishly. Elizabeth could see that he had gotten over being upset with Jessica for suspecting him of being the drug kingpin.

"I'm feeling pretty stupid about not just telling you that day you asked," Seth confessed. "If I had, you and Liz wouldn't have had any reason to distrust me. I could've helped you, and maybe things wouldn't have gone as far as they did. I guess it's just something I wanted to keep to myself, something I didn't want everyone to know about me. But I can trust you guys to keep a secret, right?"

"Of course," Jessica promised.

Elizabeth laughed. "Trust Jessica to keep a secret? You've got to be kidding!"

"I resent that, Liz," Jessica said huffily. "I can keep a secret if I absolutely have to. I didn't tell anyone about the delivery-service phone messages, did I?"

"Just me and Mom and Dad and Steven and Adam," Elizabeth pointed out.

"Well, it doesn't count if you just tell people who live in the same house with you," Jessica reasoned. "OK, Seth. Spill the beans!"

"I write mystery novels in my spare time," he began.

"Under the pen name Lester Ames," said Jessica. "Yeah, we already know *that*."

"Well, my first book was published recently, and it's selling really well," Seth went on. "My publisher's so happy about it that she gave me a contract for five more books—and a big check as an advance!"

"Oh, Seth, that's wonderful!" exclaimed Elizabeth. "I'm so proud of you!"

"Wow, a big advance," Jessica breathed. "So, how much was it? Five figures or six?"

Elizabeth winced. "Jess! Don't be so nosy!"

"It was a generous amount. That's why I've been treating myself to some new toys lately." Seth patted the Mazda's steering wheel. "But it's not like I won the lottery. I have to come up with plots for five more novels!" He looked worried. "Do you guys have any ideas?"

"I know," Jessica announced. "How about a story about a gorgeous blond sixteen-year-old who works at a newspaper office and helps solve a major crime?"

Seth rubbed his chin thoughtfully. "Not bad," he commented. "The title could be *Elizabeth Wakefield, Super Reporter.*"

Elizabeth smiled. Out of the corner of her eye, she could see Jessica bristle in the back seat. "That's *not* what I had in mind," Jessica informed Seth. "Liz didn't have anything to do with busting this drug ring!"

"Oh, I get it. You're absolutely right. Maybe a catchier title would be *Jessica Wakefield, Eavesdropper Extraordinaire,*" Seth joked.

"Very funny!" snapped Jessica. "Just remember, if it weren't for me, things would have worked out very differently tonight."

"Yeah," agreed Seth. "If you'd had *your* way, I could have spent the rest of my life behind bars!"

"Well, just think of all the time you would've had for writing mystery novels," Jessica retorted.

"Truce, truce!" Elizabeth called out. She was glad to see that Jessica was regaining her old spirit after the night's ordeal. Elizabeth looked at her watch. "We have just enough time to get to the Dairi Burger before it closes. You guys want to stop there?"

It was one subject Seth and Jessica were able to reach a consensus on. After all the excitement, everyone was starving.

"What a night," Seth declared as he parked the car in the Dairi Burger lot.

"You mean, what a *month*," Elizabeth corrected him.

"Right," he said. "Let's hope the rest of the summer is a lot quieter."

"Come on," said Jessica, hopping out of the Mazda. "This is Sweet Valley. Nothing ever happens here!"

Elizabeth smiled ironically. "That's right. Drug rings, murders, undercover agents. This must be the dullest town on earth!"

Seventeen

"How do you feel about going back to the office so soon after . . . ?"

Elizabeth didn't finish her question, but Jessica understood her meaning: so soon after the previous night's nearly fatal encounter with Bill Anderson, alias Greenback, the murderous drug dealer.

It was Tuesday morning, and the twins had just been dropped off in front of the Western Building by their mother, who had given them a ride because the Jeep was still parked near the Box Tree Café.

Standing on the sidewalk with Elizabeth, Jessica looked up to the top of the seven-story building. Despite the warmth of the sun, she shivered, remembering how perilously close to the edge she had stood and how Bill had cried out as he lost his balance and plunged to the ground below.

"I feel OK," Jessica replied at last. "It's daytime and I won't be alone. Everybody will be at work." *Everybody but Bill*, she added silently to herself. *And with him gone, there's nothing to be afraid of.*

"Well, I think you're incredibly brave," Elizabeth told her sister. "If I'd had to go through what you did last night, it would take me at least a week to recover!"

"You went through almost as much as I did," Jessica pointed out generously. "You were in just as much danger up there on the roof."

"But we both came through all right. I guess all's well that ends well," Elizabeth remarked as they strolled toward the entrance.

"I don't know about that," Jessica said once they were inside the lobby. "I mean, it seems to me that there are some aspects of this story that aren't over yet."

"You mean because some of the drug ring members might still be at large?"

Jessica smiled slyly. "No, I mean because I never *did* find out what happened with Maggie and Frank and Craig!"

Elizabeth laughed. "I bet she stayed with her rich husband."

"I bet she threw it all away for the poor but handsome country club pro."

"You'll probably never know," Elizabeth told Jessica as they stepped into the elevator. "I guess some mysteries aren't destined to be solved!"

Jessica enjoyed the hero's welcome she received from her fellow *Sweet Valley News* employees when she arrived at the office. She was a little disappointed that Mr. Robb hadn't arranged some kind of party for her, but she supposed she understood that people were not exactly in a festive mood. Everyone had been pretty dismayed to learn the fate and true identity of their former colleague, Bill Anderson.

Even better than a party, though, was the big article Seth was working on for a special edition of the newspaper. It was all about the bust of the drug ring, and included an exclusive exposé of Bill Anderson's criminal past.

"I'm putting the finishing touches on the big story," Seth told Jessica, catching her and Elizabeth on the way to their office. "Tell me what you think."

He handed Jessica the text of the article and the black-and-white photographs that would accompany it. She was pleased to see that one of the pictures was of her!

"I think *this* photo should be centered right in the middle of the page," she told him. "And enlarged, if possible. Also, would you try to squeeze my name into the headline?"

Elizabeth giggled. Seth rolled his eyes. "That's what I get for asking, I suppose!" he said.

Just then, the door to the newspaper office opened. Rose, the former receptionist, walked in.

"Rose!" Elizabeth exclaimed, a smile brightening her face. "You're back!"

The three gathered around a beaming Rose. "Mr. Robb called me first thing this morning and explained to me what had been going on around here. He offered me my old job back," Rose confirmed. "And, was I ever happy to take it! Unless . . ." She put her hand on the receptionist's telephone console, which had been returned to its original place on the big desk at the entrance to the newsroom. "Unless *you* want to stay on at the phones, Jessica."

Jessica's eyes widened. She backed away from the telephone, her hands held out in a posture of self-defense. "No, thank you," she said, shaking her head vehemently. "*Never* again." Chased by Elizabeth and Seth's laughter, Jessica made a beeline for the sanctuary of the newspaper morgue. "I think I have some filing to do!"

The most exciting stories ever in Sweet Valley history...

FRANCINE PASCAL'S

SWEET VALLEY Saga

☐ **THE WAKEFIELDS OF SWEET VALLEY**
Sweet Valley Saga #1
$3.99/$4.99 in Canada   29278-1
Following the lives, loves and adventures of five generations of young women who were Elizabeth and Jessica's ancestors, The Wakefields of Sweet Valley begins in 1860 when Alice Larson, a 16-year-old Swedish girl, sails to America.

☐ **THE WAKEFIELD LEGACY: The Untold Story**
Sweet Valley Saga #2
$3.99/$4.99 In Canada   29794-5
Chronicling the lives of Jessica and Elizabeth's father's ancestors, The Wakefield Legacy begins with Lord Theodore who crosses the Atlantic and falls in love with Alice Larson.

Celebrate the Seasons
with SWEET VALLEY HIGH
Super Editions

You've been a SWEET VALLEY HIGH fan all along—hanging out with Jessica and Elizabeth and their friends at Sweet Valley High. And now the SWEET VALLEY HIGH *Super Editions* give you more of what you like best—more romance—more excitement—more real-life adventure! Whether you're bicycling up the California Coast in PERFECT SUMMER, dancing at the Sweet Valley Christmas Ball in SPECIAL CHRISTMAS, touring the South of France in SPRING BREAK, catching the rays in a MALIBU SUMMER, or skiing the snowy slopes in WINTER CARNIVAL—you know you're exactly where you want to be—with the gang from SWEET VALLEY HIGH.

SWEET VALLEY HIGH SUPER EDITIONS

		®
☐ 27650-6	**AGAINST THE ODDS #51**	$2.95
☐ 27720-0	**WHITE LIES #52**	$2.95
☐ 27771-5	**SECOND CHANCE #53**	$2.95
☐ 27856-8	**TWO BOY WEEKEND #54**	$2.99
☐ 27915-7	**PERFECT SHOT #55**	$2.95
☐ 27970-X	**LOST AT SEA #56**	$3.25
☐ 28079-1	**TEACHER CRUSH #57**	$2.95
☐ 28156-9	**BROKENHEARTED #58**	$2.95
☐ 28193-3	**IN LOVE AGAIN #59**	$2.99
☐ 28264-6	**THAT FATAL NIGHT #60**	$3.25
☐ 28317-0	**BOY TROUBLE #61**	$2.95
☐ 28352-9	**WHO'S WHO #62**	$2.99
☐ 28385-5	**THE NEW ELIZABETH #63**	$2.99
☐ 28487-8	**THE GHOST OF TRICIA MARTIN #64**	$2.99
☐ 28518-1	**TROUBLE AT HOME #65**	$2.99
☐ 28555-6	**WHO'S TO BLAME #66**	$3.25
☐ 28611-0	**THE PARENT PLOT #67**	$2.99
☐ 28618-8	**THE LOVE BET #68**	$3.25
☐ 28636-6	**FRIEND AGAINST FRIEND #69**	$2.99
☐ 28767-2	**MS. QUARTERBACK #70**	$3.25
☐ 28796-6	**STARRING JESSICA! #71**	$2.99
☐ 28841-5	**ROCK STAR'S GIRL #72**	$3.25
☐ 28863-6	**REGINA'S LEGACY #73**	$3.25